ALL YOURS

JA'NESE DIXON

PUBLISHING

TABLE OF CONTENTS

SNEAK PEEK: PLAY TO WIN

Rules are meant to be broken, especially when it comes to this curvy chef and infamous playboy.

Miya Montgomery is the head chef and one-fifth of Southern Soul, a family-owned soul food restaurant. On the heels of a nasty breakup, Miya welcomes the shift in ownership and preparation for expansion. That's before her brother, Kamal, calls home, his best friend, Dean.

Dean Wellington arrives in Houston, ready to consult the Montgomery family through its management transition, not expecting Little Miya to be the curvy bombshell who steals his heart on sight.

Ignoring their chemistry is impossible. Dean's sweet smile and steamy eyes scorch through

Miya's clothes and her objections. However, her tattered heart is counting his casualties, refusing to be Dean's next victim.

Kamal has a strict rule concerning his baby sister: Hands off. But since when has Dean met a rule he didn't want to break. And Miya's finding it harder to ignore his independence and southern charm.

Dean's hell-bent on making their own rules, and Miya's worried that when he's had his fill, he'll leave her with an irreparable heart. But their late nights have her willing to play with fire, praying...she doesn't get burned.

ALL YOURS

"Hello, I'm Miya Montgomery, Executive Chef of Southern Soul Houston. It's a pleasure meeting you." My heart gallops even though I rehearse my new title a million times a day. I extend my hand, pretending for the millionth and one time just to hear it again.

I swirl around in a circle like Julie Andrews in the *Sound of Music.* This is my kitchen.

I'm about to burst. I fold over, holding on to the edge of the table, and run in place, squealing until all the air is out of my lungs. To say I'm happy is an understatement. I'm fucking fantastic. And the f-bomb is required because I earned it. My brothers voted and offered a trial run. But I'll change it to permanent in no time.

Accepting this position could seem evident since it's my family's restaurant. Still, my brothers—Kamal,

Rashaad, Demetrius, and Quan—put me through the pacers to prove I'm capable of running this kitchen like our mother. And I can. They'll see when we start testing with a Sunday brunch series next month.

I'm alone in the kitchen, inspecting every drawer and cabinet. We're closed on Sundays, but Kamal— my oldest brother and head Montgomery on this project—asked me to meet him this morning. I didn't expect a totally new kitchen with stainless steel appliances—the prep station, stoves, refrigerators—all new everything.

A fresh bubble of excitement boils over, and I can't control myself. I'm dancing to the music in my head, squealing again. Ass jiggling, boobies swinging until a soft gasp cuts through the air, and I freeze in place.

"What are you doing?"

I spin around, facing the voice. "Minding my business. Who are you, and how did you get in here?"

An unfamiliar man with familiar dark brown eyes stands in the doorway, well, fills it is more like it. I need to adjust my bra and smooth out my clothes. I can only imagine how I look because everybody can't handle these curves. Still, I'm more interested in getting some answers.

He steps closer, and I slide a chef's knife from the block, pointing it in his direction. A smolder descends over his eyes, and the temperature in the room heats up a notch.

"Don't make me turn you into two wings, two legs, and a breast." I flick my wrist with each cut to show him I'm not playing.

"Baby Miya is all grown up." His teasing gaze sends a shudder down my spine.

"Baby Miya? Only my brothers call me that. Who are you?" I ask while simultaneously trying to place his face—the strong jaw, dark brown hair, and tanned skin—but there's no way I'd ever forget those eyes. They're too distinctive. Too dark. Too knowing. And like a self-defense expert, he claims the knife, pinning my back against the refrigerator.

"You should be careful—you could cut someone."

"I think that was the point, handsome," I bite back, and he smiles, and it's as tasty as cream cheese icing on warm carrot cake.

"How'd you get in?" I ask, moving to free myself, and his grip tightens, not meant to harm. The contour of his biceps through his expensive suit jacket tells me that he's cut, and if he wanted, he could lock me down. But the hold of his strong hands feels more like a caress.

"I'm here with Kamal."

Our chests rise and fall. Inhale, exhale.

Every cell in my body stands at attention. Heart

pounding. Lungs demanding. Eyes shifting, openly assessing one another.

His lips, one thin, the other plump, both tempting, hover inches from mine. The scent of spearmint rushes between us every time he exhales.

Caught between cold steel and a rock-hard body, I'm suddenly tongue-tied, which is unlike me. But what's a girl to do with a man like this?

I lick my drying lips, and a deep groan vibrates through his chest and mine, as if in agony. A wave of emotion crosses his face. I'd call it pleasure if I knew him better—or maybe determination as he steps back, freeing me. He replaces the knife in the stand, angling his body towards the door.

"I'm on my way. I need to settle a few things at the restaurant." Kamal talks on his cellphone in his own world.

My eyes jerk to the door. I didn't even hear him. Thank God he didn't walk in and see us. My eyes find *his* again. Kamal sweeps the room, continuing his conversation, opening and closing each of the refrigerator doors.

"Jayda, just make sure you're packed. And babe, you don't need a million bags. We're only going for a couple of days."

I shake my head and laugh. There's no way Jayda's packing light—it's not in her. She's a beauty vlogger and all the way around a glam kind of woman. Three days means at least three outfits per day, accessories, shoes, and makeup. I chuckle. Kamal better drive the SUV.

The stranger's penetrating eyes drag me back.

"So, what's your name?" I ask.

"Dean."

"Dean." I repeat his name a few times, resting a hip against the prep station.

"Hey, Baby Miya, sorry about that." Kamal gathers me to his chest and kisses my temple. "Do you remember Dean? He used to come home with me sometimes for holiday breaks."

"Not really." With four popular brothers, all of their friends are a big blur to me. "Miya Montgomery, Executive Chef of Southern Soul. It's a pleasure meeting you." I extend my hand, reciting my rehearsed introduction, and it feels so damn good.

"Dean Wellington. The pleasure is all mine." The smoky tone in his voice matches the flames in his eyes as he steps forward. He takes my hand in his, and a zap of awareness overtakes me. But instead of lingering, I firmly shake his hand and step back, rejoining my brother. "Nice grip."

"Thanks."

"What do you think of the new kitchen?" Kamal asks.

I blink out of Dean's trance, glancing up at my brother. "It's perfect. How'd you manage to make this happen overnight?"

"I didn't. Dean did." Kamal smiles and returns to examine the new equipment. He opens and closes drawers and then runs his fingers across the handles of the new pots and pans. "I've been working with Dean for months to get this place up to par."

"I busted a move or two when I came in here and saw this place sparkling like new money." I glance over at Dean, curious, and find his waiting eyes. A trail of something sweet ripples through me. But the last thing I need is another man in my life. The ones I have are driving me mad, including Kamal, as we struggle through this transition. "So, what's next? The dining room could use an update too."

"That's on my list. After this, I'm thinking about taking a trip to North Carolina to inspect Southern Soul Raleigh."

"Raleigh?" I gather him in a quick hug. A trip to visit the other location is a major development for Kamal. When our parents divorced, Dad took over Southern Soul Raleigh, and Mom resumed her work at Southern Soul Houston. But we've never been active participants in the operation of the other location. "I'm so proud of you. Dad must be thrilled."

"Don't get gushy. I'd visit it because it's a sound

business decision. We can't honestly take on this job without seeing the state of it firsthand. The numbers look good, but..." Kamal shrugs a shoulder, as if not convinced, leaning back against the sink. "Which brings me to today. I called you here because I want you to spend some time with Dean."

Heat flows through my body, remembering the feel of being pinned against the refrigerator beneath Dean. The two of us alone together isn't happening. Not at all.

"And why would I do that?" I ask.

"I want to exploit this feeling of newness. New management. New equipment. New staff. I want the two of you to craft a *new* menu for Southern Soul. We'll test it—"

"*Pause*. You think I need him to create a new menu?" My thumb flicks towards Dean, now resting with his back against the wall, observing us. A slight smile replaces his neutral expression. "No offense."

"You're good." A hint of humor dances in Dean's eyes, and it takes everything in me to look away.

"Kamal, I don't need a babysitter."

"No one said anything about a babysitter, Miya. I hired Dean—"

I halt the words with my hand in the air. The imaginary party balloons in my head pop like they're taken down by a firing squad.

"You don't have to say he's a babysitter for it to be true." I should have known there was a catch. Kamal towers over me by at least six inches. But it doesn't stop me from walking closer with a hand placed firmly on my hip. "You do realize that's what a head chef does?"

"Miya." He grips my wrist and removes it from my hip. "There's no need for you to huff and puff."

"I'm not huffing and puffing... but I'm about to." I swallow around my disappointment.

Kamal has always encouraged me to pursue my career. He helped me get internships and called in several favors when it was time to secure my first real job. But here he is acting like my old bosses and my ex—like I'm delicate China prone to breaking—and this shit hurts.

"Miya, love, get out of your head. He's here as a tool, a guide, that's it." Kamal throws up his hands as if he's harmless. But he's a wolf covered in faux sheep's wool.

"Don't give me that damn smile. I'm not buying it." My voice cracks, and I'm embarrassed. This is precisely why I didn't join the family business. They don't see me as a professional chef, but Baby Miya, and I'm tired of it. I march to the door, pissed. "I'm out of here."

"Miya, please don't leave." Kamal catches up,

placing his hand firmly on my shoulders. "You're the best damn chef we could have hired. Hiring Dean isn't a reflection on you or your position. It's a standard process. When a business makes a transition, they hire outside consultants to make the process as smooth as possible for all parties involved."

I shake my head. "A major chain, maybe. But this is a mom-and-pop business. Southern Soul is family-owned and operated. *We* don't hire consultants to handle *family* business." I yank from his grip.

"And that's the problem," Dean says from behind Kamal. "To take Southern Soul to the next level, you can't continue to operate like a *family* business. No disrespect."

I glance back. "None taken."

"Miya, your work is respected in the industry. You've worked from a commis chef to a sous chef, to your recent Head Chef offer from Torsion. No one doubts your expertise or ability to manage a kitchen."

How did he know? I turn around and face Dean. I didn't tell my brothers or parents about the offer I received from Torsion in Austin. I never wanted to work in other restaurants. I wanted to work in this kitchen—my family's kitchen—my whole life.

"You had an offer from Torsion?" Kamal asks, blocking my view of Dean. "Why didn't you tell us?"

"It didn't matter."

"It *does* matter." Kamal cups my face, and he searches my eyes. He knows how I've fought in other kitchens to be respected as a woman, and a curvy Black woman at that. I did it all to work here. "I'm sorry, Baby Miya."

I nod. It takes everything in me not to shed a tear. I got the nickname Baby Miya because I'm the youngest and the only girl in a family of five children.

A single tear motivates my brothers to move heaven and earth to seek a remedy. I love my brothers, but right now, what I need more than anything is for them to see me as an adult.

Not Baby Miya.

That I can handle myself professionally as a chef and not my abilities to huff and puff and blow all this shit down like a damn baby. Which means if I want this position permanently, they have to trust me, without a consultant standing over my shoulders.

I'll show them. No tears allowed, I remind myself, stepping back.

"I'm listening."

Kamal tips his head to the side. "Look, I was working with Dean before we asked you to take over the kitchen."

"I'm a team player. I think hiring him is a waste of money, but that's why I cook, and you make the decisions."

"Miya…"

I turn my back to Kamal and face Dean head-on. That jab is intentional. We called Kamal back to help us take over the family restaurant and do it the right way. This is my family's business and our legacy. I don't need this handsome consultant to tell me how to cook my Mamma's food. Dean knows my resumé, but he'll see soon enough, he's not needed here. But I'll play along, for now.

"What do you have in mind?"

CHAPTER 2

THE SEXY SMILE on Miya's face comes with the ringing of bells in my head. Kamal gives me a pleading look, and I brush the tip of my nose.

It's our universal sign for *I got you.*

"I need to make a quick call. I'll be right back." Kamal leaves me to convince the very pissed Miya to work with us, not against us.

"What will it take to send you packing?" she asks when Kamal clears the door.

"Trying to get rid of me already?"

"You and I know the head chef handles the menu. I don't need an assistant to do it." The smug look on her face sends a challenge my way, and challenges are my specialty.

"I guess that's why it pays to listen to the extent

of my contract for this project because I wouldn't assist you. It's the other way around."

Her head snaps back, and a flutter of laughter spills out. "You're cute and delusional. Answer the question. What will it take?" She crosses her arms, and her plump breasts perk up higher, serving as a temporary distraction.

I took this job to help my best friend. Little did I know Kamal's kid sister—he affectionately calls "Baby Miya"—isn't a baby. Baby Miya is a curvy woman with a brown-sugar complexion, a round face framed by curls, and hypnotizing almond-shaped eyes.

"Dean?" I blink and Kamal's back.

"Give us a few more minutes."

He heads back out, leaving us alone in the kitchen. I flew into town this morning to walk through the first phase of our renovation before approving the next stage in the dining room and to meet with Miya.

To prepare, I did what I do, researched her history in the industry. Her reputation is impeccable. Her lasting impressions with past chefs boil down to her loyalty to the brand, her kitchen skills, and the energy she infused into the work environment. Not one chef reflected negatively on her employment, and all would gladly hire her again.

That's rare. Cooking is such a personal experience. And to multiply it by thousands and recreate that magic repeatedly takes dedication, and what few realize is it takes heart.

Chefs have to love people in the kitchen and in the dining room. Chefs have to sacrifice days and nights and relationships. And chefs do it all in hopes of one day running a kitchen or their own restaurant.

So, when Kamal called me and told me about the family business's shift, I told him I'd walk him through every step. He's not a chef on paper, but quiet as it's kept, the man can cook his ass off. And if the man decides to bless a grill, he can convert a vegan to a carnivore. I've seen it with my own eyes. I wonder if Miya has the same ability in the kitchen.

For a man with many talents and the power of persuasion, Kamal is concerned about the petite woman standing in front of me. Miya's revered passion in the kitchen is on full display. And somehow, Kamal's worried about converting his biggest fan, and the core of his heart, Baby Miya.

"I'm here to visit a few local restaurants, to get a feel for the most popular establishments."

"That's easy. The Breakfast Klub, Houston This is Soulfood, Just Oxtails..." She runs down the list. "But nobody serves food like Southern Soul."

"I appreciate your confidence, and I believe you, but that's not the point of my little excursion."

"What's the point?"

"You'll have to join me to find out." I glance away, only for a moment, with a chuckle. "You asked for my plan. That's the beginning. Eventually, we'll have a new menu to present to Kamal before he starts running his test Sundays. The customers will help us filter it down to the final version. Are you in?"

My question hangs in the air, accompanied by the sound of our breathing and Kamal's voice in the distance. He hired me while I'm in-between two large projects, one in New Orleans and the other in New York. But this is important to him, so it's a priority for me.

I'll have to extend my stay, book a hotel, and reschedule a few appointments. No doubt, I'll pay for it, but the opportunity to spend some time with *Baby Miya* is growing more intriguing by the second.

Her neck rolls, causing her bangs to block my view of her beautiful eyes. A slow smile spreads across her face as she runs her tongue along her teeth.

"I'm not on the menu, Mr. Wellington."

The roll of my name off her tongue does some-thing to me. And something tells me she knows it.

"So, is that a yes?" I pull out my phone to review

my calendar. Channing and my team will have a fit once I call with the shift in my schedule.

"Did you hear me?"

"Yes, Miya, I hear you loud and clear. I'll remember that." I extend my phone. "I need your address. I can swing by your place and pick you up around six-thirty."

"Wait, this starts tonight?"

"It's one of the reasons for my trip today. I have a reservation at the first place tonight at eight and a tour of the kitchen with the executive chef at seven-thirty. The GPS says it's about an hour from here."

Her forehead wrinkles. "Just the two of us?"

"Yep, you and me."

We exchange phones.

Her screensaver is a family portrait with Mr. and Mrs. Montgomery sitting sideways. Miya is front and center with a toothless smile so full, she's oozing joy. And the boys are behind them with matching grins. They all look so happy.

"How old were you here?"

She turns her head to the ceiling in thought. "Four, maybe five. That was our last family picture. Here." She returns my phone, and I give hers a final look before giving it back. My parents and I never took a family photo.

Kamal re-enters the kitchen as we reclaim our

phones. He gathers Miya to his chest, and the desire to hold her fills me. Then I remember I'll have her all to myself tonight.

What's wrong with me?

My eyes sweep from Miya to Kamal, and he squints as if seeing something for the first time. "Dean, this is my sister. None of your player bullshit."

Miya snorts. "Not gonna happen."

"Is that so?" Fireworks explode in my body. I hope she realizes she's playing with the wrong one.

"It is so." Then she tosses a saucy gaze my way. "You're not even my type."

"Are you challenging me, Miya?" I lock my entire focus on her.

"Dean." The warning in Kamal's voice doesn't deter me. We're adults.

Miya leaves her brother's side, walking until I can see the streaks of copper in her eyes. I slide my hands in my pockets to keep from learning firsthand if her skin is as soft as it appears.

"To challenge you would mean I care, and I don't. My priorities are Southern Soul and my family. So, let's get this done."

"Can you handle me?"

"Excuse me?" Miya unfolds her arms and plants them on her full hips. I force myself to watch the lightning crack in her eyes instead of the rise and fall of her chest.

"Can you handle working with me?" I slow down the cadence to get under her skin.

"I can handle anything and *anyone*."

Miya takes another step, and we're almost back where we started. The edible scent of her perfume fills my nose. And the thought of her handling me brings a smile to my face.

"I'll admit, you knowing my resumé surprised me, but you can find that with a basic Google search." She cocks her head to the side, mirroring the one her brother is infamous for. "Do us a favor—leave your suggestive ogling and five-dollar come-ons at your hotel."

Miya straightens my tie, and the heat from her hand penetrates my cotton pinstriped button-up shirt. Then her eyes pop up to mine. The burn in my chest is like I swallowed a tube of wasabi. It overwhelms me, numbing my senses to anything, and everything, except her.

"Are you done, baby girl?" I love nothing more than a woman who knows how to handle her tongue.

Miya rolls her eyes, stepping back. I follow her as if we're dancing.

"I can assure you, what I have in mind will exceed

your five-dollar threshold. And for the record, I *love* challenging women."

"That's where you're wrong. I'm not here to challenge you, but to send your ass home." She wags her finger. "Four brothers and a headstrong father means I know every trick in the book. You gotta come better than that. And for the record, I'm not other women."

"Yes, ma'am."

Miya's whipping a red cape in front of a bull, and for the first time in months, I feel alive.

Flying coast to coast, handling my clients' needs, overshadows any resemblance of a personal life. I know the hospitality industry. I eat, sleep, and breathe everything needed to make a restaurant thrive. But right now, I don't give a damn about Southern Soul Houston or my other clients.

All I see is Miya Montgomery, and for that reason alone, she's not like other women. She has blood rushing through my veins and my nose wide open. Something tells me this curvy bombshell's about to wreck my life.

"I'll leave you guys to your business." She speaks to us, but her eyes are on me. "You don't have to pick me up. I'll meet you there." She turns to walk away again but stops short and spins back. "You're officially in my way, and what Miya wants, Miya gets. So, don't unpack your luggage." She winks and double taps my chest. "I'll see you at six-thirty."

The view of this woman from the back stops me dead in my tracks. Her little warning is cute. I can't recall the last time a woman put up a challenge *and* laughed in my face. That shit doesn't bother me one bit. It's a fucking turn on and will only make my victory sweeter.

I watch until she clears the door, and sirens are blaring in my head. Yet, I hear a soft whisper, a warning: Miya is Kamal Montgomery's sister.

His baby sister.

His only sister.

"Hands off." Kamal's eyes are on me, no doubt reading my mind. "You hurt her, and you'll draw your last breath."

I acknowledge his warning with a nod. That's a bridge I'll have to cross at another time. Plus, we both know I'm not looking for a relationship.

Kamal's a magnet, drawing life to him, including myself and Emmitt Booker. We met in junior high school, and our friendship continued through college and into playing professional football. But it was sometime in college when the three of us made a pact to remain single for life.

We each have our reasons. Kamal's issues with divorce. Emmitt's upbringing in the foster care system. As for me, it wasn't my parent's divorce, but their dysfunctional relationships afterward. The examples I've seen in "committed" relationships" haven't been the best, and I don't want to add to the staggering statistics.

Living single agrees with my work schedule and lifestyle—I'm a modern-day nomad. The three of us, self-proclaimed, life-long bachelors, have traveled the world. And I can work without restrictions. But lately, I feel off, like a part of me is missing, and I don't know what it is or where to find it.

I've vacationed.

I've partied.

I've worked.

The weight of not knowing feels suffocating until I walked in and saw Miya dancing around in the kitchen, without music, without a care in the world. I try to recall the last time I was happy enough to dance without reservation, without music, and with my damn self. That shit must be dope.

I stop before opening one of the ovens and ask Kamal, "When's the last time you've looked forward to something?"

"Today." He beams, sitting on the table. "Jayda has this thing she started with Reese since they moved to Houston. She calls it 'making memories.' And it's all about them having fun in a new city, familiarizing themselves with the local attractions. But to me, I see my city through their eyes. The zoo, museums, restaurants. Last weekend we went to the spa."

"You at the spa?" I laugh. Seeing Kamal in a relationship makes me wonder if he plans to actually settle down. It's mind-blowing.

"Yep, me and my little ladies. I took Lillian, Reese, and Jayda for the works, and…" His eyes glaze over. The light of the memory covers his face, and for a moment, I let myself wonder what it must be like to have people in my life that I can count on other than Emmitt and Kamal.

My mother has a new family. My father travels the world cooking and bedding every woman he can. I have no siblings, a few close cousins in New York, and have my trusted staff. But I spend the majority of my time alone or with my boys—Emmitt and Kamal.

Kamal is the most sensible and responsible of us. He has his parents, siblings, and now, Jayda, his girlfriend, and her daughter Reese.

"You're a lucky man."

"I'm a *blessed* man," Kamal corrects.

"Sounds like you're about to break the pact."

"I would in a heartbeat if I thought Jayda was ready."

I'm surprised by his admission. I wait for him to

explain, but my friend seems to be far away in thought.

I'd never intentionally cross him. I'd never intentionally jeopardize our friendship. But electricity hangs in the air, and the heat of her touch lingers on my skin, long after Miya's departure.

Is it selfish to want more?

CHAPTER 3

I moved home for this. Boxes cover my house, and with a slice of pizza in my hand, I decide to start in the living room. The last thing I need is junk food, but with my life overrun by men, I need carbs. I take a bite and toss it on a paper plate. Then I pop in my buds.

Carbs and music.

Today I need some Drake. I select a playlist, and I start unboxing. The move from Chicago was unexpected. I always knew I'd come home, but my plan was to return, having made a name for myself in the culinary world. Maybe a husband and a baby or two. In this fictitious world, I'm in my mid-thirties, my goal weight, and I can stand up to my brothers, parents, and especially my eldest brother Kamal. But none of this is true, and the little incident at Southern Soul shows I'm far from my ideal situation.

The music plays, and I shift through the boxes of my life. Then I hear a song, and I know it's the one. I tap repeat on *Jungle* and crank up the volume letting the melody drown out my thoughts.

"Miya!" Hands grab my shoulders. I jump and start swinging. "Stop."

"What are you doing, trying to scare the shit out of me?" I pull out a bud, and Rashaad removes the other.

"No, why do you have on noise-canceling head-phones with your door unlocked?"

I stare at the door and Rashaad, my brother. "My bad. I can't think with these boxes everywhere. Y'all just dropped them in the middle of the living room."

"You said to leave them." He smiles, bringing me in for a hug. "You stink."

I laugh. "Shut up. What are you doing here?"

"Mom has Lillian, and I thought you could use some help. Since you're allergic to boxes."

"I am." I lie with a straight face. Then we're laughing again. "If I can get the living room, kitchen, and bedroom cleared, I'll be a happy woman."

He eyes my set up on top of a box. "Where's the pizza and the wine?"

"Kitchen counter, help yourself." He zig-zags

until he disappears into the kitchen. "What about Demetrius? Is he coming?"

"Yeah. He said give him a few."

I stick the buds back in my ears, lowering the volume. When I have a problem, I need repetition to see a clear path.

"Where's the meat?" Rashaad says, but I can barely hear him, so I turn the music off.

"I'm trying to watch my figure."

"With pizza and wine?" His brow lifts.

"Look, keep the judgment out of your voice. I'm taking baby steps."

"Knock, knock." Quan, my baby brother, stands in the doorway with a frown on his face. "Yo, your door is unlocked. Did you forget this is Houston?"

"Rashaad did it." I laugh, and he peeks around the corner, offering Q some pizza.

Q weaves through the boxes, not stopping until I'm pulled into a tight hug.

"What's up, Baby Miya?" He kisses my cheek. "Bring me a slice."

"It's cheese."

"Cheese? Where's the meat?" He looks over at me.

"Look, y'all got houses. Don't come to my house complaining. Eat the damn pizza and unpack a damn box."

Q looks over at me like I've lost my mind. "Oh, you done went to Chi-Town and lost your mind."

Rashaad laughs in the kitchen. "I got you. I ordered some real pizza and beer."

"Welcome back to Texas, baby." Q smacks a kiss on my cheek, and I rub it off.

I almost forgot what it's like to be home with my brothers. I'm the only girl with four older brothers—Kamal, Rashaad, Demetrius, then Q.

"Eh, why are all of y'all in here with…"

"The door unlocked." We say in unison and laugh.

Demetrius steps in with the pizza. "I tipped the driver and locked the door."

"Damn, how many Montgomerys does it take to lock a door and unpack?" I ask like it's a riddle.

Q brings the party. He clears the table and spreads out the food pizza, wings, and beer.

"Toss the buds and press play. Let's get this house unpacked." Demetrius says, and I send my music to the wireless speakers.

They gather around the island, and I watch them. I didn't have to get movers or find a place to stay, nor will I have to unpack alone. My brothers look out for me like that. I glance at the time, and it's after nine. I wonder for a second what Dean thought after I didn't show up. Then I push him out of my mind.

"Yo, where's Kamal?" Q asks.

"He took Jayda on an overnight date," Rashaad offers.

"Am I the only one surprised by this Jayda situation?" Q leans against a box.

The others shrug. I'm not surprised. Jayda's a beautiful woman, inside and out. She and I have hung out a few times, and I see us doing it more now that I'm back in town.

"I'm not. What surprises me is he's in a relationship with her? I never saw that one coming." I say, stacking my family pictures on the coffee table.

"And a kid?" Q adds. "But Reesie Piecie is the truth."

They chuckle. Jayda and Kamal started dating a few months ago, and her four-year-old daughter has my brothers wrapped around her little fingers. Uncles 'Shaad, D, and Q jump at her every command.

"Yeah, they suckered me into a trip to the zoo and the museum district on Thursday." Demetrius, our New York Times bestselling author, adds.

"They?" Q asks.

"Lillian and Reese." Demetrius clarifies, opening another box.

I laugh this time. "Wait, they called you?"

"Yes, and said 'Uncle, it's free all day.'" He chuckles. "They want to visit one more time before it's too cold. Those girls are grown."

Our family of six—Mamma, the boys, and I—has grown. We have Kamal with Jayda and Reese. Rashaad and his daughter Lillian, who lives with him full time now. Mamma and Daddy back together. It seemed like it's the perfect time to return home until I discovered Kamal's little plan with Dean.

"Did y'all know Kamal hired a consultant?" I ask them, sitting on the cleared couch.

"Dean." Rashaad nods.

"When was someone going to tell me?" I expect Kamal's call any minute because I chose to unpack instead of meeting Dean tonight. I don't need Dean's help, and the sooner he realizes, the sooner he can go back to wherever he came from with those steamy eyes.

"We asked Kamal to handle it. He's handling it." Q shrugs. "You have to let the man do his work in peace."

Q runs one of the hottest clubs in Houston. Rashaad owns and manages a real estate agency. Demetrius writes full time. Before returning home, I worked full time as a chef in Los Angeles, San Francisco, New York, and my last gig was in Chicago. At the time, turning over the issue to Kamal seemed like the right thing to do since he has always handled these types of matters for the family.

I won't go against Kamal, but Dean can stay out of my kitchen.

"What do you know about him?" I sip my wine, waiting to see which brother will speak up first.

"He's Kamal's business partner with Emmitt." Rashaad sits on the love seat. "I've known him for years. He's a decent guy. They send clients my way from time to time."

"Q?"

"Dude's a *Wellington*." He drags out the name like I should know it. "The hoteliers, restaurateurs."

"As in *Isaac Wellington*."

"Come on, Baby Miya, this is supposed to be in your food world. He's a fucking restaurant rock star."

I lean forward. Isaac Wellington is like the Bobby Flay of the world. He owns restaurants on almost every continent.

"And Isaac is Dean's father?"

"Yep. But Dean's no joke. That dude consults the biggest restaurant chains in the country." Q downs a bottle of water.

"Then why is he here?" I ask.

Rashaad answers, "Kamal. The three of them usually trade-off personal projects, tagging each other in and out of the process."

"We're just moving from Mamma to us. Why do we need a consultant?"

"Why not?" Q asks, and his knowing gaze has me uncomfortable.

"We've always handled Southern Soul as a family is all I'm saying."

"Huh." Q dangles his water loosely in his hand. "Stop beating around the bush. Either Kamal said something or Dean rubbed you the wrong way."

"Kamal wants me to work with Dean to recreate the menu," I tell them.

"That sounds reasonable," Rashaad says. "It's normal to review and update business policies and practices with a change of ownership."

"Rashaad, bringing in Dean to help me recreate a menu is like Kamal hiring someone to oversee the purchase of a new building. Why hire someone if we have you?"

"So, he stepped on your toes?" Q asks. Q's the shit talker. He's fast, he's raw, and he decodes bullshit faster than a speeding bullet.

"No, Q. I don't need help creating a menu."

"And you're pissed." Q smiles.

"It's like me with writing. I know I can write a story, but I still have my editor. Two minds are better than one, and he sees what I miss. Why not work with the best to ensure you're producing the best?"

Demetrius walks over and joins us in the living room. "How about you tell us what happened instead of giving us the edited edition?"

"What?" I ask.

"Stop giving us the highlights and tell us the details."

"Shut up, Q." I throw a pillow. Then I tell them about meeting with Kamal earlier today.

"The kitchen's done?" Q asks. I nod, and he whistles. "That man is like a restaurant whisperer."

"A what?"

"He helped me renovate my kitchen when I did the expansion. I called Kamal, and he called Dean. Dean said, let me make a few calls. My shit was up and running in weeks when others said it would take months."

"And the quality?"

"I don't play about my shit, and I don't cut corners—Dean's legit. Now the question is, what did he say that has you trying to kick his ass out?"

"I didn't say anything about kicking him out."

"You don't have to." Q points like *I see you*, and I look away.

"How did the meeting at Trios L'Amour go?" Demetrius asks, not missing a beat.

"I didn't go."

"What?" They sing in unison.

"I didn't go."

Q chuckles. Then he outright laughs. "Oh, sign me up for the Kamal and Miya showdown." He folds over, laughing.

Rashaad shakes his head. "Did you talk with Kamal?"

"No, he's on his date with Jayda."

"You know that vein that pops in his forehead. That one right here." Q points, and he's howling with laughter. "That shits gonna be throbbing."

"Q?" Rashaad and Demetrius try to stop him, but he's on a roll.

"Leave it to his Baby Miya to buck. Oh, King Kamal's going to roll some heads when he gets back."

"Get out, Q."

"Don't kick me out because you fucked up."

"I didn't fuck up. I just made an executive decision. I'm the head chef. I'm in charge of the kitchen." Now I'm nervous. Maybe I should have gone. I look over at Rashaad. "Is Q right?"

"Pretty much. Kamal's investing at least two million in this project. And if the kitchen is renovated in a day and a half..." Rashaad shrugs. "You should have gone or called as a professional courtesy."

I glance at my phone, and it's after midnight. "I don't care how much Kamal's paying Dean. Why do I need help cooking my mamma's food? I learned to cook her food before I could see over the prep station. What can he tell me about dishes I can create with my eyes closed?"

"But the point of this is to get better, right?" Rashaad asks.

"I guess. I'll have a talk with Kamal."

"What can we do?" Demetrius asks.

"Meet me at Southern Soul Wednesday. I'll show him I don't need a consultant in the kitchen."

"Ah, shit. How much can I pay for a ticket to the showdown?"

"Q!" we shout.

"I'm going to the club. I know when my advice is not welcomed." He kisses my cheek and smiles in my face. "I hope you're ready, Baby Miya."

"Q, you're a pain."

"Maybe. But running a business isn't the same as considering the kitchen alone. The same way you want to handle the kitchen your way, Kamal wants to oversee this transition. You can't ask for the man's help then dictate how he should do it." He shrugs. "But what do I know?"

He hugs the others and leaves, but his words stir in my mind. Rashaad kisses my cheek and heads home.

Hours later, Demetrius and I sit on opposite ends of the couch. I love all of my brothers.

Kamal's more like my father. He raised us after our parents divorced. He made sure we had our homework done, cooked dinner for us, and put us to bed. Most girls had parents in the stands at volleyball games and cheerleading events. I had Kamal.

Rashaad is our peacemaker. He knows how to navigate between our personalities. He's levelheaded, responsible, and he manages to see through our differences diplomatically. He always brings the parental oversight and warmth. That was until his divorce. He's still as loving, but there's a steel-like approach that he's never had before.

Q is Q. Loud, boisterous. Talks shit but tells the truth. He says Dean's a restaurant whisperer. Well, Q's the club whisperer. His place is killing it, and he's on the heels of opening another. He's all laughs and jokes until it comes to his club and his family. So tonight, I know he was trying to school me. Trying to help me to see, I made the wrong move.

Then there's Demetrius. We've always been the closest. He's the middle child, and I'm the baby. His silent strength has a way of making me feel invincible. It always takes me by surprise when I read his books. For someone so quiet, he sees so much.

"Are they right?"

"Yes. That was a brash move. You want Kamal to

see you as an adult. This will not help you do it. He'll see it as you pulling a Baby Miya stunt."

"Fuck. Will you come on Wednesday?"

I know he's about to leave town. He usually hides in his cabin for a few weeks when he's preparing to write a new book.

"I can hang around a few more days." He extends an arm, and I crawl over and lean into my brother. "How are you doing with all of this? The move? The restaurant? Corey?"

"I've wanted this for so long, and I almost have it. I'll have to remind Kamal. For him, it's a business deal. For me, it's all I've ever wanted." I smile up at him.

"Lead with that, and he'll fall at your feet." Demetrius gives me a slow smile.

"Bullshit."

We laugh, and I push up to find another box. We crank up the music and get back to work. This is one of Rashaad's rental properties. It is almost four times the size of my apartment in Chicago.

"And Corey?"

"He's out." I look down at the box instead of my brother. This break up was long coming. They kept telling me Corey was no good, and I kept trying to see the best in him. But there's something about walking in and seeing another woman in your bed.

She was sleeping like a baby in the bed I bought.

On the sheets I bought.

On my fucking pillow.

Before, I argued and fought with Corey, but that stole the fight right out of me.

I left Chicago on Kamal's private jet. Rashaad gave me this house. Q kicked Corey's ass, and Demetrius went to Chicago and packed my belongings. Then they approved, giving me the position of my life in the kitchen where I learned everything.

My brothers are the best in the world, and now I have to figure out how to convince Kamal to leave the kitchen to me.

"What am I going to do?"

"You aren't a gratuitous hire. Kamal knows you're capable of handling the kitchen. You'll have to show him that his decision was right and that you're the best chef for the job."

"But how?"

"Put your buds in, and you'll think of something."

I nod, scanning my playlist, selecting another Drake track. "Are you out too?"

"Nah, I'm here until you get this place in order. You'll need some rest if you're planning to face the dragon."

I laugh, hugging him. I could have easily taken

that head chef job at Torsion in Austin. But I want to be here. We're all taking a chance here. However, nobody, and I mean nobody, can cook my mother's food better than me. So, Kamal and I need to get on the same page.

"You're a real one. I'll go put on a pot of coffee."

Demetrius chuckles, breaking down a stack of boxes. The man lives on coffee. I press play and crank it up. The thoughts in my head ride the beat, and I keep it real with myself.

Q's right. Kamal stepped on my toes and kicked me in the shins. I thought I'd slip in my new role, show them, and they'd crown me the new queen of Southern Soul Houston.

I make Demetrius a cup of coffee and pour another glass of wine for myself. And an unexpected sight descends over my senses. Dean's smoky eyes and my immediate attraction to him.

I sigh.

"You good?"

"Yeah. Here."

He takes a sip and leans against the counter beside me. "This is good."

"It's a flavored bean from HEB." I was surprised by the extensive selection and grabbed a few bags. "My living room looks almost normal."

"You need a few more pieces to make the space

look like you. But overall, this is a nice house." He breaks down more boxes and tosses them by the front door. "How's that plan coming along?"

"It's not."

"Why not call him and reschedule?"

"I deleted his number from my phone." I cringe.

"Miya."

"I know. He just rubbed me the wrong way." Or the right way, but I can't tell my brother that. We're close but not that close.

"Make sure you tell Kamal about not going before Dean does. You don't want him blindsided."

"I will." I pull out my phone and send a group text.

Family meeting Wednesday morning at ten. Southern Soul. Breakfast on me. I drop my phone to the table.

Demetrius checks his messages. "Got it. And what's the plan?"

"I'll do what I do best: cook. I won't have to tell him. I'll show him. He'll be off the high of his trip with Jayda." I nod, letting the idea take form. "I'll cook Kamal's favorite dish and show that I have the kitchen covered. That he can use Dean elsewhere."

We bump fists, and with that, we get back to unpacking. I smile with the feel of victory settling around me.

CHAPTER 4

MIYA STOOD me up last night, *and* she gave me the wrong number. I tap the end of the table and sit back. Her not showing up shocked me.

"Mr. Wellington, when are you going to stop accepting new projects?" Channing asks, sitting in the seat across the aisle.

"We're not having this discussion. Did you update the files with the notes I dictated while in Houston?"

"Yes, sir." She shifts under my direct gaze. "I sent the care package to the crew, and Mr. Martinez called with his gratitude for the bonus."

I nod. His crew was exceptional. "Update their internal rating to a five. I think he has a small crew in Northern Louisiana and Southern Oklahoma. Follow up with him and get the details. I'd even pay extra to transport his Houston team."

For the rest of the flight, I walk through the locations visited in the past week. I started in New Orleans I'm prepping them to move forward with franchising. Then Shreveport was a walkthrough of a construction site in need of help for a homeless shelter and soup kitchen. And I ended in Houston. It's unreal how much the team accomplished in thirty-six hours. We gutted, renovated, *and* staged the kitchen.

I split my time between DEK Ventures—a privately held investment firm with Kamal and Emmitt—and consulting with restaurant owners worldwide. But with the new DEK charity initiatives, I'm only accepting domestic consulting gigs this year.

"I need to return to Houston late Saturday for an early start Sunday."

"Yes, sir. Here are the files for the next phases."

"Give me a moment to review them. And get me some coffee, please."

Channing moves across the aisle, and I spread out the files. This is my life. Moving from city to city. Strategizing, repairing, and building restaurants, and on rare occasions, I have to tell the ugly truth. My clients pay me well to be honest, knowledgeable, and on time. Last night was the first time I arrived late to an appointment in almost ten years. I waited outside the restaurant for Miya, thinking it was traffic only for her not to show.

But her not arriving made the rest of my time in Houston easier. I don't have to worry about my lungs burning and my heart racing.

I turn my attention to my work. New York is another personal project. My cousin is renovating a building he recently purchased. I sent an architect over around the holidays. Now we're ready to move forward with reimagining the interior structure into a conference and a virtual business center.

This is the first time I'm working on this type of project. He asked me to oversee it, and it is stretching my knowledge of design and layout. It's not as enjoyable as restaurants, but it's still gratifying to watch the transformational process. To turn a building from one thing to another.

"This is Dean," I answer my ringing phone, laying my head back.

"You in New York yet?" Emmitt asks.

"Naw, man. I should land in a couple of hours. Why, what's up?"

"A friend of a friend asked if I have a friend," he says.

"What?" I sit forward.

"Violet Masters invited me to a private showing of her upcoming movie."

"Damn..." I sing with a laugh. "You got it like that?"

"Shit, she had her people call my people. And I was like, this is on some Hollywood-type shit. But I'm down."

"What did you say?"

"Fuck if I know. I zoned out at Violet Masters."

We laugh harder, and Channing chuckles. She knows the drill. Emmitt is the craziest man I know. He'll have you laughing until you can't breathe. He should be a fucking comedian. But he's promised his team another three years on the football field.

"How did she see you?" I ask.

"Press conference after the game. Guess she likes football."

"Ah...shit. Playa... playa..."

"They couldn't tell me shit. I walked out of there like George Jefferson."

I fold over. "Man... She probably saw that ten-million-dollar signing bonus."

"Yeah, who hasn't. I got all kinds of folks coming at the woodworks. I have my assistant designing my Mike Jones cards. Ya boy is hot, and now they have their hands out."

We die down and discuss the details of his contract.

"So, you want to roll?" he asks.

"Yeah, what time? I need to do something other than work."

"Bet. I'll get the details and send a car to get you. Are you staying at The Wellington?"

"Yeah. I'll be there for a couple of days before heading back to Houston. Then back to Nola. When will you land?"

"We might touch down around the same time. Can you hang around for me?"

Channing's shaking her head.

"Yeah, man. Private, right?"

"You know it."

"Bet, I'll see you in a few."

I disconnect the call. "Channing, I appreciate your attempts to keep me focused and on track. But there are a few people who operate outside the scope of clients. Kamal, Emmitt, and Pops. When they call, move shit. Understand?"

"Yes, sir."

She starts clicking on her keyboard. I have a meeting in New York, but I need to eat some good food, find a good drink, and laugh my ass off with Emmitt.

I spend the rest of the flight clearing tasks,

sending emails, and reviewing my schedule with Channing. The chime of my phone interrupts, and I check my messages. It's in our group thread.

I open and see a snapshot of a business card. I zoom in but don't recognize the name. The organization is a little league.

Yo… is this for the football summer camp? Emmitt jumps in first.

Yep. We got the green light, Kamal responds with a brown fist bump.

DEK Ventures wants to work with inner-city charities starting with a fully-funded summer football training camp. It's Emmitt's pet project. He'll relocate to Houston for the summer to oversee it.

D drinks on me!!!

I drop a couple of moneybag emojis and a fist bump. I'll gladly drink on Emmitt's dime. He can afford to cover the drinks.

Drinks? What are y'all doing 2 nite? Kamal asks.

Landing in NYC. I add, watching the crew prepare for landing.

Where you at? Emmitt asks Kamal.

Vegas w J.

Aahh shit, y'all making it official, Emmitt adds.

I shake my head. If only he knew.

Nah, man. Just relaxing without Reesie.

This dude is 2 minutes from… Emmitt adds a ring emoji.

I throw in a few laughing emojis.

Touching down, I add, gathering my jacket.

Me 2.

Be safe, Kamal says with a brown emoji throwing up two fingers.

It's not long before Emmitt is heading to the waiting car. We grasp hands and tap shoulders.

"What's good with you, man?"

"Tired. Where are you staying?" I ask, climbing in the SUV. The moment I'm with my boys, I relax. I'm free to be myself.

"I had my assistant move my reservations to The Wellington." Emmitt passes his bags to the driver. "How's Southern Soul coming along?"

I run a hand over my face, not sure how much to tell. "The project is going well, but when's the last time you saw Baby Miya?"

"She must have been in junior high, maybe high school."

I wag my head.

"What's that mean? She looks good? She looks like Kamal in a skirt?"

I laugh. "Man, you're a fool. She's…"

Emmitt leans into the door giving me a stern look. "Don't do it."

"Do what?"

"What you're thinking? You know Kamal and his damn rules." He laughs.

"But you break every fucking one!"

"Yeah, I know, right."

We laugh, and I turn to watch the city go by.

"Man, what the hell? Don't tell me you're joining Kamal."

"What are you talking about?"

"He has a whole woman with a child. So much for his rules." Emmitt shakes his head. "I bet they'll be married by this time next year.

"I see her sticking around. But married?" I ask, then Kamal's words come back, and I think Emmitt's right. He'd marry her now if she said yes. "What do you think that is?"

"What? The falling in love part or the marrying part? I don't know, but I have too many options to settle for one."

I sit back and think about his response. I guess the real question is, what would make a man give up all his options to have one woman. For the life of me, I can't wrap my head around it. My parents divorced when I was in junior high, and Pops never remarried. He always cautions me on settling down. He says men with our net worth aren't meant for one woman.

Pops now has a woman for every city he has a

restaurant. But I can't see my life like that. At some point, it must get tiring. *Right?*

The closest I've come to being with one woman is when I used to mess with my nanny. Pops arrived home early from a trip and caught her giving me head and fired her on the spot. That was my last nanny.

"Tell me about Baby Miya. Slim. Thick. Slim-thick."

"She's thick in all the right places. Sassy-ass mouth. Quick-witted. Beautiful eyes."

A visual of her settles over my mind—she's dancing around in the kitchen with her ass bouncing and full breast. I shift in my seat with the thought of her, and I remember the feel of her body beneath mine.

"Beautiful, *huh*. Big brown eyes?" he coos.

"Nah, almond. She has this bang that–"

Emmitt punches my arm. "Man, Kamal's gonna kick your ass from Houston to New York and back."

"What?" I throw up my hands.

"Talking about beautiful almond eyes." Emmitt batting his lashes, and this shit is awkward.

"What? You asked."

"He wanted to kill me for fucking his publicist. He. Will. Kill. You. Over Baby Miya."

"I didn't do anything."

"Not yet. But your beady-ass eyes and Romeo tone says it's only a matter of time. Take my advice."

"What's that?"

"Don't do it. It's his kid sister."

"I won't."

"It's his *only* sister," he drags out.

"She's not interested anyway." I run my hand through my hair.

"You must have a death wish? You already tried?" Emmitt is laughing, and this shit isn't funny.

"No, she was supposed to meet me last night–"

"What the fuck, man?" He's sitting forward amped. "This is going to be good. He's always worried about me. Issuing warnings when he should be watching your ass."

"You are enjoying this a little too much."

"I am. Y'all treat me like I'm the fuck boy."

"And you are."

"Okay, maybe. But I'm not over there sniffing behind, Baby Miya." He laughs, slapping his leg. I should have kept my thoughts to myself. "Look her up on Facebook. I want to see her."

"Nah, man. Let it go."

"Fine…" He opens the app.

I could stop him, but I don't. I want to see how she looks in pictures too. Maybe save a picture or two for myself. He finds her by looking at Kamal's profile.

"*Dayum*!" His head jerks back like Smokie on Friday. "Hey…Baby Miya."

"Give me the phone. Let me see." I snatch his phone. "Fuck…me."

Miya's standing in a mirror taking a selfie. The dress fits like a second skin. Her seductive glare jumps through the phone, and I'm struggling to keep my shit from standing up. I pass his phone back and think about concrete, steel beams, glass for windows, anything to keep from thinking about Miya in that black dress.

"Exactly. You better enjoy it, and I'll say some real dope words at your funeral."

"Man, I can't stand your ass."

"Here lays my Caucasian brother, from another mother." This fool has his hand over his heart, and I'm dead. "He thought he had swag. But his ass didn't have shit once Kamal found him lus*ting* over Baby Miya."

I'm howling. Rolling back and forth because the shit is hysterical.

"Let us pray…" Emmitt has his hands up like a baby Buddha.

And I'm done. I can't stop laughing. Emmitt is praying that I got all the ass I needed in this lifetime and the next. That the Man lets me in because I'm a brotha coated in white chocolate. That I'll leave him in my will to inherit the Wellington billions because he is my best friend, and he warned me—several times.

We finally settle down, and I look over. "Maybe it's a good thing she didn't show up."

He snickers. "And she stood you up. *Jesus*! Let us pray."

I laugh all the way to The Wellington as Emmitt prays that I am blessed with some game. And I'm anointed by Brother Emmitt to go forth and smash.

Amen.

CHAPTER 5

IT'S BEEN A WEEK, and I'm sitting outside Southern Soul gathering my thoughts. The place is transforming. We have a paved parking lot, fresh paint, and new glass in the doors. But today's visit isn't about the renovations. I'm here because I called my firsts family meeting.

The level of anxiety I'm feeling is unreal. I don't want to come across as disrespectful or egotistical, but I have to stand up for myself. Demetrius made me realize I should have followed through with meeting Dean because my beef isn't with him. It's with being clotheslined with this whole consultant situation.

I'm not going to lie, but I'm not telling the whole truth—that I wanted to throw the middle finger to Kamal and *his consultant*. I can't say that, or I'll come off as the brat they make me out to be. But I meant to be shady.

It is what it is.

Kamal and Jayda stayed away for a few extra days. I used the time to unpack and get a new license and tags for my car. I spent the first day watching my phone for a text or a call about me ditching Dean. But I got nothing. I figure he didn't say anything to Kamal, which makes the man I'm trying to forget somewhat unforgettable.

He didn't rat me out. Why?

Curiosity sent me to my trusted advisor, Google. On everything, it was in a moment of weakness. Those smoky eyes kept popping up in my mind. His whispers across my skin. The feel of being pinned under his hard body.

I groan.

My brothers painted a picture of Saint Dean, and Google confirmed it. I feel like the scum of the earth because I acted childish, giving him the wrong number, deleted his number, *and* I stood him up.

I have a list of rebuttals for Kamal, and I run through them, stopping and starting over every time I hear my voice quiver. Then I notice a couple in a car across the way at a drugstore. They're face to face, not kissing but a whisper away.

The man gets out and circles the car extending a

hand. She looks up at him, and I see the affection from over here. She steps out and immediately cups his face kissing him, and I turn away from their private moment. The tenderness makes my heart jealous.

How do people find *that*? They walk inside, and I pretend I'm not staring. But how can I not stare? Love oozes from them, and I wonder: *Why not me?*

Why can't I have someone opening my doors and whispering love across my lips? Why can't I have a man so into me that all he sees is me?

My heart stalls. My eyes burn. My soul yearns.

But that's not for me.

It can't be.

I've tried, and I keep finding lame-ass men professing to want me, yet I find random chicks in my bed. Like what the fuck, do I have, please invite your side chick to sleep in my bed written across my forehead. I mean, how disrespectful can a man be? And I pick the bold ones, cocky, fine. The ones that flaunt, taking pictures for the world to know, *I'm not enough*.

I brush away tears.

I consider the source. Is it because I miss Corey? Is it because I regret my decisions? Is it because for all of my ambitions, this one is as old as my aged journal, stuffed in a memory box in the back of my closet?

I want *that*.

I want my own somebody.

But Corey's infidelity makes me see that I might have to settle for my career. Because I can't go through that shit again.

So, it's time to let him go. I've moved from Chicago, and I'm not letting him follow me.

It's done.

I'm over it.

"Move the hell on, Miya."

I scan my phone looking for my new favorite song. Leave it to Mariah Carey and Jermaine Dupri to underscore the end of this week. This is officially the emancipation of Miya Montgomery.

No more bullshit.

I gotta shake it off!

I press play and tap repeat. The beat is catchy, and I bounce side to side. I close my eyes, singing to every no good ninja that's used my heart like a doormat. I'm a good woman, and Corey knows it. That's why his ass is calling and texting.

Then the chorus hits, and I turn that shit up. You can't tell me I ain't Mariah as I shake off the games, the drama, and the heartbreak.

I bounce and scream like my ass can sing. But I can't care more about others than I care about myself.

Corey's out.

Now I have to walk in Southern Soul to confront Kamal and my brothers about this whole Dean situation. It's another step in my emancipation. My freedom from giving a fuck about people and situations that don't give a fuck about me.

I have to do this for me.

I let the song repeat, and I close my eyes. The thing about making your own soundtrack is you have to feel the beat and the lyrics down to your soul. Repeating until you embrace the confidence and vibrato of the performer. That's why I love Drake. He gives me the melody of a singer but the attitude of a lyricist, which I need to walk in a room looking like me.

Big lips.

Wide hips.

Big hair, don't care.

I'm going to listen to MiMi one more time and hit Drake a couple times before going inside. With my prescription in place, I close my eyes and take my medicine.

A knock on my window causes me to jump. I look over, and it's Catrina—the hostess and new manager.

I've known her most of my life, but the age difference used to get in the way. However, returning home, I see we have more in common than I realized. The longing gazes she sends towards my brother Rashaad are familiar. Something tells me we are kindred spirits.

I unlock the doors. Catrina sits in the passenger seat, and I turned down the music.

"Everything okay?" she asks, bringing the scent of food with her.

"Yeah, trying to get my head on straight. Are they ready?" I glance over, looking inside the restaurant.

"Yes. I set them up in the kitchen the way you asked."

"Thank you, Cat. Let me finish taking my medicine, and I'll be there." I hold up my phone, and she chuckles.

"What's the prescription today? I might need a dose."

"*Shake it Off* by Mariah Carey."

"That's a good one to reset."

I nod. "And Drake, *Nonstop*."

"Oh, I like that. Are you about to listen to that one?"

"Yeah."

"Mind if I stay?" she asks.

"Not at all."

I tap play, and we jam. I don't have time for any misunderstandings. It's time to get my respect.

I rap, and Cat's hyping me up. Demanding my respect. Reminding people, there's no one like me. Stating the facts for the record. When the hook drops, we rap in sync, pointing fingers at our targets. Snapping fingers swaying because the 808 demands a mean, nasty rock.

I thought the announcement was all I needed to move into this new season of my life. It seemed like the perfect segue from Chicago back to Houston but hiring Dean tells me Kamal doesn't trust me.

I'm the right woman for the job.

I'm the right Montgomery for the job.

The parking lot concert continues, and when the song is over, I'm ready to face my brothers. It's time to show them I'm not here to play.

"BABY MIYA." Kamal stands and gathers me in a hug. He kisses my forehead and reclaims his seat. I hug each of my brothers, then my parents stopping once I'm in front of them. There's a construction crew working in the dining room, but we're alone for the most part. I look around at the newness and begin.

"I'm ready to resume the role of Executive Chef immediately."

"The role is yours," Kamal says with a smile.

"No, Kamal, it isn't. The executive chef handles all matters concerning the kitchen. And I respect all that you're doing to update Southern Soul—the changes to the building, the staff, and this kitchen. But from this moment on, this should be my domain."

The others exchange glances.

Demetrius gives me a reassuring wink, and I continue.

"Starting with hiring Dean. I don't need help with the menu. In fact, I like it the way it is."

Kamal rubs his eyes and levels his gaze. "Baby Miya—"

"Chef Miya," I state for the record, and the tension in the air hikes up a notch.

Kamal continues, "Chef Miya, hiring Dean isn't about merely recreating the menu. It's about—"

"Taking Southern Soul Houston to the next level."

I look up, recognizing the voice, and my heart leaves the building. Dean and I occupy the same spots as last week, except I'm not dancing, and he's not smiling.

"This is a family meeting," I say.

"Does anyone object to me attending this meeting?" Dean asks with his gaze locked with mine.

No one speaks.

"Kamal might need you out there. But I'm good in here." I state.

"There's no way to make the adjustments needed to ensure profitability and growth if we don't start in the kitchen."

"I don't need a *stranger* coming in here telling me how to cook my mamma's food."

"And that's where you're wrong again." Dean removes his jacket and grabs an apron off the hook. "See, what you're missing is fundamental. It's the heart of every restaurant, even this one."

He unbuttons the cuffs of his shirt and rolls back his sleeves. The colored tattoos capture my attention. He lights a fire under the skillet. Then the man stands at my station.

Dean talks, and I hear not a single word as the man expertly wields the chef's knife like a Master Chef. He cuts the chicken into perfect portions. Seasons the flour. He double-dips each cut in a buttermilk and egg mixture. Then he releases the pieces into the hot grease without a splash. The aroma of fried chicken fills the air, and all I see is the man's mouth moving.

He whips the buttermilk waffle batter adding a

few extra ingredients from the refrigerator. He's talking and cooking, and we're all spectators.

Can this man be any sexier? Standing in an apron, in my mamma's kitchen, cooking our signature dish.

Dean swirls a butter and maple syrup concoction over the plates with a dusting of powder sugar. He adds two hot waffles, a slab of grass-fed butter, topped with two pieces of fried chicken, and adds more powdered sugar. Then he cleans the edge of the plate with a fresh towel and slides it across the station.

"Chef." He extends a fork to me with a gruff tone and firm grip in his jaw.

I want to look at the others. What the hell is happening here? This dude just mind fucked me in my own kitchen.

I take the fork and cut into the dish. The moment it touches my tongue, I moan, and my eyes find his. I see his rage, but I also see something else, and before I can give it a name, it disappears.

"Chef Miya, I'm here to help your family. Either you assist me or get out of my way. But don't waste my time." He removes his apron and turns to Kamal. "I have another meeting."

Dean leaves the kitchen, and I'm right behind him.

CHAPTER 6

Kamal mentioned this family meeting in passing. I thought it was the perfect opportunity to clear the air with Miya. Walking in on her "I don't need Dean speech" had me cheering for her gumption and despising her dismissal of my contribution. I'm flying back and forth to help my friend and his family build this business, and she sees me as—how'd she put it— a *stranger*.

I storm outside, pissed. I'm known to keep my cool, but coming from Miya, it cut deep. But it's not until I reach the parking lot that I remember I didn't drive. My rental is scheduled for delivery in another hour.

My head drops back, and I exhale, reaching for my phone.

"Do you need a ride?" Miya asks.

I stop, not facing her. "No, thank you."

I ignore her huff taking a deep breath. I'm tired. I glance at my watch, wondering if I have enough time to run to the hotel and rest before visiting Trios L'Amour. But I don't. Then I remember the bench. I spin around and freeze. She's still here.

Today she's dressed in a pantsuit. Her curly fro is eye-catching and draws my eyes to her face, and ultimately her lips.

"You look surprised," she teases.

"I thought you left."

"I didn't."

I'm not naturally irritable. I deal with too many people, too many moving parts with projects, and deadlines to sweat the small shit. But this woman gets under my skin in the worse kind of way.

I step around her and walk over to the bench outside the restaurant. That's when I notice we have a crowd.

"Why are they staring at us?"

"Ignore them, and they'll eventually find something else more appealing."

"And Kamal?" I glance back at her.

Miya shrugs, "He's sizing you up."

I laugh and sit. She hands me my jacket and sits beside me.

"I think I owe an apology."

My head snaps to her.

"What?" She shrugs. "I had this grand speech in my head. I'd tell Kamal to fire you. My mom to release the reigns. My brothers, I'm an adult. Stand back, watch me do my thing. And you walked in."

She huffs again, and her bangs flutter.

"You ruin a kick-ass speech. It took me forever to get it all together. I listen to Mimi ten times and Drake like twenty, and you walk in all fresh-to-def, cooked my dish—which was bomb as fuck—dropped the mic, and walked out like kiss my ass bitches."

Who is this woman?

I'm pissed, but I'm smiling. I feel it the moment it spreads across my face, and she's having this conversation with herself.

"The maple and butter sauce was…I bet Kamal ate it all. It's his favorite dish, and now I'll have to make it like that."

"Is this your apology? And who are Mimi and Drake?" I wiggle my hand in a circle because all of this, all of her, wrapped in this delectable package assaults my ego, my mind, and yet I want more. And even after a week of hanging with Emmitt cracking jokes about my imminent death, I know she's different. Death doesn't seem so bad if I get a chance to kiss those lips she's mindlessly chewing on.

Her head cocks to the side. "You don't know Mariah Carey and Drake?"

"Yes, but what do they have to do with you apologizing?"

"I listened to their songs. And I said I *think* I owe you an apology. I haven't decided if I *will* or not."

I laugh, and I'm sure this woman is crazy. "Please explain this debate."

"No, because you already think I'm crazy. I can see it in your eyes. So, let's table the apology and tell me this plan of yours. The one to visit the other restaurants."

"I'm visiting area restaurants for research over the next few months."

"Three months?" Her face wrinkles, and it's adorable. "It doesn't take that long to visit restaurants."

Suddenly I'm back on the football field, and I see the play before I throw the ball. I revise my plan.

"The alternative is spending *every* Friday, Saturday, and Sunday with me." I smile. "And you have to agree *before* I have my team reshuffle my calendar."

She huffs again. "Do it. That'll take us down to two months. But I don't expect you'll last that long."

"Is that so?" I could pass the time away, sparring with her.

"It's so, Mr. Wellington. When are we starting?"

"Tonight. I need your address and number." I pass her my phone for the second time. "The *real* ones."

Miya enters her information, and I send her a text. Her phone chirps, and she shows me the screen.

"How should I dress?"

"Formal."

"Let me get back inside before they join us."

I glance over my shoulder. I never realized how big her brothers are until this moment. "I'll be there are six-thirty."

"I'll be ready." Miya stands, and I wish we had more time. "Don't let this little victory go to your head."

And with a wink, she's gone, and I'm a goner.

THE ANTICIPATION of seeing Miya and having her to myself tonight had me mindlessly floating from moment to moment. Now, I'm sitting outside her house, alone with a head full of questions. But none are more critical than the coin toss between my friendship with Kamal and my interest in Miya. Respecting my best friend's request to stay away from his sister or following the speck of hope that there's more to Miya than her beauty and her resume.

I rub my chest, and it's as if she lit a small match inside that's usually cold. A place I closed off before I realized that hiding is the breeding ground for isolation, and ultimately, loneliness—a place I colorfully mask as success.

Unable to decide, I remove a quarter from my pocket and snake the metal between my fingers.

I'm here because Kamal asked me to assist him with this transition. I expected long hours, constant traveling, and calling in many industry favors to make it happen. What I didn't expect is Miya. She impressed me on paper, but in the flesh, she's ten times better.

Kamal's command to leave his sister untouched is warranted. He and Emmitt know the highs, lows, and secrets of my life. He has a right to be concerned about my unexplainable attraction to his little sister.

I stare at the coin. Heads, Miya. Tails, Kamal.

I flip the coin in the air, catch it, and smack it on the back of my hand. The porch light flicks on, and I slowly peel back my fingers, tilting toward the yellow glow.

Tails.

"Fuck."

I PEEK THROUGH THE BLINDS, watching him sit in the car. I showered and dressed. I run back over to the mirror, fluffing my hair. I had my beautician cut a bang, and I like how it draws attention to my eyes. My black dress travels the curves of my frame, ending at the top of my knees, and leaves plenty of wiggle room for me to enjoy dinner.

"This isn't a date. This is business," I remind myself, adding an extra coat of lipstick. "Stop! This is operation *Get Rid of Dean*."

I follow my orders, dropping the tube in my purse. I give him his props for earlier, but I still want him out of my kitchen. Then I realize there's no need to wait for him since this isn't a date. So, I activate the alarm and swing open the door, and almost drop dead.

Dean's mouth drops open, startled mid-knock. "Miya, you are…stunning."

The word escapes in a whisper, and I catch it, bottle it up, and tuck it away to examine later when my knees don't feel so weak.

"And you, Mr. Wellington, will have the women falling all over themselves." His dark suit is paired with a black shirt and no tie.

"Shall we?" He extends an elbow, and I take it.

We walk to the car at the end of my driveway. Dean opens the door, and I slip inside. He removes his jacket, tossing it in the back seat.

"Mind if I kick off my shoes?"

"Do your feet stink?"

I burst out laughing. "No! Why would you ask someone that?"

"We have an hour drive. If your dogs are kicking, it will kill all the effort you put into preparing for our night."

I cut a look at him. "Who says I prepared for tonight?"

"Red bottoms. Killer dress. And not a single curl is out of place."

I snap my mouth closed. He smirks, turning the engine over, and the car purrs to life. Dean plugs the address into the navigation system and pulls away from my house.

We make it to the highway, and I'm bothered by the silence. "You don't listen to music."

He shrugs. "Not really. I prefer to think while I drive. But you can."

"Think about what?" I tilt, facing him.

"In general, or right now?"

"Either, both."

"I'm thinking about all the decisions that led to this moment. And…my goals for the night." His eyes leave the road briefly before darting back.

"And those are?"

He sighs. "It's hard to explain. I like to line up my expectations, so I know what to look for, then clear a path to see the situation for what it is."

"Hum." I think about his words as the car slows to a stop, thanks to traffic. "Sort of like having a goal but giving yourself permission to be present."

"Exactly."

His eyes hold mine until a blaring horn pulls him away.

"What about you? What are you thinking about?"

"Nothing as profound as you, Mr. Wellington."

"Try me."

I laugh. "I'm thinking about the dessert menu."

His laughter spills over, and I'm stunned by how it transforms his face. "Dessert. Okay. What are your favorites?"

"Oh, that's like asking my favorite shoe, or my favorite star, or my favorite song. I have a list of favorites in my life. I can't ever seem to decide on one, so I've decided to love them all. Which contributes to these thick thighs, an epic DVD collection, and more shoes than I care to count." I fold my legs in the seat. The chill of the air conditioning and the comfort of the luxury bucket seats make for a great ride, minus the traffic. "Mind if I use your jacket?"

"Not at all," he says, a notch above a whisper.

I drape his jacket over my bare legs and ask a million and one questions. His favorite color is orange. His favorite vacation spot depends on the time of the year.

His responses are thoughtful. His laughter is rare. His smiles are frequent.

"Why do I feel like we've met before? Kamal said you visited, but did we meet?" I ask, rolling my head to look his way.

"We did. One year for spring break and another for Thanksgiving."

I sit up. "Wait, I remember. You guys played football."

Memories of that Thanksgiving rush forward. "I was in junior high."

"Wow. That puts a new perspective on it." He

chuckles. "If you don't mind sharing, how old are you now?"

"Twenty-seven." I sit back.

"No husband or kids."

"No, not yet." I watch the scenery pick up as we reach the edge of the Houston city limits. "What about you? No Mrs. Wellington?"

"No." The finality in his response makes me want to ask more until I realize we're here.

I slide my shoes back on as Dean walks around the car to open my door. I hold up his jacket, helping him slip inside, smoothing down the collar, and for a moment, neither of us move.

I clear my throat. "How do you enter these types of situations?"

"I pretend I'm a customer."

"You're just full of wisdom," I joke, retaking his elbow. We walk to the entry, and instead of looking around, I watch him. The way his dark gaze sweeps the room. "I thought we have a reservation."

His dreamy eyes look down into mine. "We do. I want to see how they move the guest in without a reservation and check out the waiting area."

There's a covered sitting area before we reach the front doors. Once inside, there are cushioned benches for guests to sit comfortably while they wait. The people around us don't seem to mind the estimated hour seating time.

I make a mental note to discuss adding seating to Southern Soul. Our Saturday crowd usually wraps the building. This means sometimes standing for thirty to forty-five minutes outside. Offering seating would definitely help to upgrade our customer experience.

We step forward, and I follow Dean's lead, observing the restaurant as a customer. The lighting. The background music. The proximity of the bar to the sitting area. The aroma in the air.

"Why do you think the uniforms are different?" I whisper.

"They're probably bar only waiters, and the others are for the dining room."

I nod, watching a waiter take a drink order. Customers laughing and talking. "The wait is part of the experience."

"Exactly." Dean winks as we step closer to the podium. He asks for the chef, and minutes later, we're moving through the restaurant.

I give myself the same drill: stomach in, shoulders back, chest up. Think tall thoughts. Head high. Get your Beyoncé on. Like magic, my mind plays *Diva* by Beyoncé, and I strut. The click-clack of my heels on the oak floor blend with the soft music, underwriting the track in my head.

I know how to dress my size eighteen, and you'd think I'm a twelve. Snatch the waist, fluff my hair, a killer heel, all play into my look. But adding Dean on my arm is extra, a moment when a dude's swag matches my swag, and the shit is sexy as hell.

Hair bouncing, hips swaying, with a gentle smile on my face. From my peripheral vision, I see the man with my hand sandwich to his side, feeling the rhythm of our cadence. It takes the sight of several bucked eyes to keep from snapping my fingers and spitting a verse.

We reach the other end of the room, stopping at a pair of double doors leading to the kitchen. Dean crosses me to hold the door open. I glance back and find all eyes on us.

Food suspends in midair. Mouths hanging open. Conversations drop to a whisper, and I don't blame them. Dean is a beautiful man.

Chest to chest, I pause, holding his dark gaze. "Do you always attract this much attention?"

"It's not me, but the beauty on my arm." I squeeze past, brushing my chest against his, appreciating the heat in his eyes and the trail of desire running through my veins. Then I face the kitchen.

"Mr. Wellington." A tall man steps forward in his chef's hat and jacket.

"Chef Pierre, it's good to see you again." They

shake hands. "This is Miya Montgomery, the Executive Chef of Southern Soul." Dean's hand relaxes on my lower back, and our eyes hold for a second. The slight tilt of his mouth incites the urge to kiss away that smug expression. And I know, right at this moment, that I want to see if this chemistry between us is real.

"Miss Montgomery, it's nice to meet you. I try to visit your place for brunch whenever time allows."

I face the chef with a smile, taking his hand in a firm shake that would make my father proud. "Please tell me the next time you visit, and I'll prepare something special." I wink, and Dean shakes his head with a chuckle.

Chef Pierre turns beet red. "I plan to take you up on that offer."

"And I'll be offended if you don't," I add.

We laugh, and he pulls us inside his immaculate playground.

The activity in the small kitchen makes me want to kick off my heels and jump in. The staff moves as one as Chef Pierre gives us a first-class tour. I make up my mind to focus on Dean and not the chef. The only way I'll get rid of him is to find an angle, and to find his angle, I need to know the man.

Skillets saluting, pots simmering, and the aroma makes my stomach growl. But it's the Dean Show that has me tuned in. He asks questions here and there, but like earlier, he listens, contributing a sentence per ten minutes because the chef loves to hear himself talk.

This reminds me of when I used to spy on my brothers. All I'm missing is music, but the sounds of the kitchen are like sonic therapy, and I'm totally relaxed. Which makes studying the stern expressions on Dean's face entertaining.

Chef Pierre takes us through the entire place when he's called to a station. "Pardon me."

Dean nods, and the chef steps away. His assessing gaze sweeps the room as if capturing each detail. I've clocked five repeats, which is a solid base to work with. It's easy to understand men once you break them down to a few core components. Their level of communication, the way they treat their mother, their vices, and their relationship history. Let's see how Dean holds up.

Dean's not a talker, but he communicates with his expressions. A subtle nod and sweeping gaze when the response registers. A slight grip of his strong jaw when he's put off. A tip of the head and lift of his eyebrows when he's surprised. I hide those for future reference.

"Does he owe you money?" I whisper to Dean, and he glances down with smiling eyes. That's a gesture he's only done a few times, but it's the one that softens the darkness in his eyes.

"No, Miya."

I glance across the room, watching the chef give a brief demonstration. "He wants to do business with you?" His head tips back and the lift of his brows means I'm right. "What kind of business? Investments? This place doesn't need renovations."

Dean faces me, folding his arms over his massive chest. He rests his chin on his fist like the thinking man.

I throw up my hands. "What? It's not like you're a wealth of information. I'm piecing this together. How else will I get rid of you? I have to know what I'm working with."

The chef returns before Dean can respond, but the humor lingers in his eyes. The ring of my phone interrupts us as Chef Pierre returns. I silence it, not acknowledging Dean's penetrating glare. Then the damn thing starts humming, back to back.

I scan my text messages, and it's very telling.

Answer the door, Miya. Corey's at my house. I stick out my tongue, and then I remember I'm not alone.

When are you going to start acting like a mature adult? When you learn to keep your pecker in your pants. But I'll have to send that when I'm alone. I wish someone would create a kiss my ass emoji or get lost, loser. Until then, I'll ignore Corey.

"It must be urgent. Do you need to take that?" The muscle beats in Dean's jaw.

"No." I swipe the screen, deleting the entire thread, and drop my phone back in my purse. Eventually, he'll get the picture. "The only thing that matters is Southern Soul."

CHAPTER 8

CHEF PIERRE and Trios L'amour delivered to my expectations. He's one of the best in the country. The fact that he's been voted Top Chef in Houston for two years in a row doesn't surprise me, but Miya's sudden silence does. She got distracted by her cell-phone, and it's as if she's pulled into a shell.

No jokes. No eye rolls. She's here, but then again, she's not.

Miya went from asking a million questions, like a curious child, to retreating deep in thought until we're seated, and she starts examining the menu. Then slowly, she reemerges, inspecting the menu with hums, and oohs, and the occasional, "that sounds good," nibbling on her pouty lips.

Now, she's sipping her wine, toying with the rim of her glass until she snaps the menu closed.

The fact that someone keeps calling her should smack a big fat X across this woman. I'm not out here looking for anything permanent, but even my causal situations must be drama free.

I figure the sender of the messages and the person calling nonstop must be her man. A woman like her can't be single, and knowing she has a man waiting for her makes sticking to my coin toss easier, in theory.

It would also keep Kamal off my ass and leave his sexy sister untouched.

But…the moments when I caught her inhaling the aromas in the kitchen with a broad smile and teasing to the point of making Chef Pierre blush, it leaves me wanting to know what else she has to offer.

"Something tells me speechless is different for you."

"I'm…trying to decide what I plan to do about you." Miya drains her glass and levels her gaze on me, holding me on the edge of my seat. Waiting to see what she says and does next.

"Me?"

She nods. "Yes, you, Mr. Wellington."

"What are our options?" I close my menu and set it aside.

"That's part of my troubles."

"Huh." I lean forward against the table. "Is there a way I can help?"

Her gaze sends desire through my body, challenging my decision to keep my hands to myself. The warmth of her arm interlaced with mine earlier was a tease for a man like me that hates samples.

"Tonight went differently than I expected."

"Chef Pierre is a master chef. From his equipment to his crew, to the menu, and ultimately the food. Be prepared to have your mind blown."

"My surprised didn't come from Chef Pierre, but you."

Surprised by her response, my breath catches. "Is this more of your 'what Miya wants' business?" I tease, but Miya's not the only one used to getting their way. I never do things by halves—I want it all.

"Maybe. My plan for tonight was to give you a hard time. But now, I'm having second thoughts."

I relax in my chair.

"Kamal, hiring you threw salt all in my plans. This was my chance to step up and show my family this job was made for me."

"How so?"

"I've worked in kitchens across the country, always with my mind set on replacing my mother when she was ready to step down. And she finally starts considering retirement only to offer the position as a temporary assignment."

I see her fight and her struggle. "It's difficult stepping into an existing brand. It's why I have clients lined up to work with me."

"I'm starting to think Kamal knew what he was doing when he hired you. And don't you tell him, at least not yet." She chuckles.

"It takes a humble person and a team player to accept what's best for others, at the expense of yourself."

"It's not like that with us. And that's the part I have to remember. My brothers want me to succeed. I just have to see what Kamal wanted me to embrace when he hired you."

"So, what you're saying? Is it cool for me to unpack my bag?" I smile, referencing her saucy threat from before.

"No, keep your bag packed. I have a few things to learn, and once I do, I plan to bump you aside," she says with a flick of her hip, rocking the chair. "You wanted me here, and I see the place. Why'd you pick it?"

"It's part of my process."

"To visit the competition?"

"Do you consider this place your competition?"

She has a way of leaning into her neck that signals

a fast comeback. I see it coming, then she closes her mouth with a wag of her finger. "This is one of those trick questions. Let me see." She taps the end of her finger on her chin, scanning the room. "To keep it real. No, we're both restaurants. So, we're both in hospitality, serving food. But the differences outweigh the similarities."

"How so?"

"Location. They're in The Woodlands. We're in Fifth Ward. Our clientele differs, but that could be an outpouring of location, culture, and food. This place is what, a French-Creole fusion?" Her eyes narrow as if really taking a look around us. "Whereas we're about comfort foods, foods that make you remember your grandmother and Sunday dinners around the family table."

"Anything else?"

"The place is packed, and that's with reservations. I'd love to see Southern Soul like this. And I know we can if…" Her words drop off. The wistful tone in her voice grabs ahold of me, and I want to make her wish a reality.

"If what, Miya?"

"That's your job, mister," she jokes, trying to pass the ball.

"Actually, it's not."

Her face bunches in confusion. "I'm listening."

"Do you always lead with that statement? You said the same to Kamal earlier."

"I might. It's how I force myself to get out of my head and focus. But don't flip this around on me. You seem to dodge every direct question." She exhales. "You have my attention, Dean. How do you see my role in this transition?"

"I see you, Miya, as the cornerstone." I let my words sink in.

"Are you bullshitting me?" The quiver of uncertainty in her voice surprises me.

"No."

"Flirting?"

"No, you'll know when I start flirting."

"Like when you pinned me against the refrigerator?" She leans forward, resting her arms on the table, with blinding heat in her eyes.

"Nah, that was to get your attention and to keep you from slicing me into two wings, two legs, and a breast."

Her head tips back, and she laughs. Her laughter lifts the cloud brought on by her cellphone, and I join in, unable to stop myself.

"Enough dodging. Answer the question."

"Why do people visit restaurants?"

"Dean…"

"Miya, answer the question. Why do people visit restaurants?"

"To eat," she rattles off, with a hint of sarcasm until she quiets again. But this time for another reason.

"This place was voted number one in the city for two years in a row, in the fourth largest city in the United States. And Miya, it starts in the kitchen. As the executive chef of Southern Soul, you have the power to turn it all around."

"So, what is it that you do?"

"I consult restaurant owners and chefs. The extent of my work runs from idea through franchising. I work with startups to families like yours moving from one generation to another."

"What does that mean? Not boardroom talk. Give it to me plain."

"Okay. I help people get unstuck and explore the best options for their business to be profitable. I explore business models, theories, and trends. But for many, it's about reworking the vision from the inside out. Then we look at the offerings, the environment, the staff, the management."

"Is that part of the reason for visiting this place?" She nods, approving the refill of her wine glass.

"Yes." Her question surprises me again.

The waiter arrives, and we order dinner. We relax

into our conversation until the food comes. The food is perfect, the service exceptional, and I'll have to email Chef Pierre first thing in the morning.

"So, what's the plan?"

"I fly out to New York in the morning, and I'll return Friday morning."

"Wait, you don't live here?"

"No, I haven't since junior high. I used to visit my mother over summer breaks and holidays until I turned sixteen."

"Is that how you met Kamal?"

I nod. "We played football together a few years, but lost contact once my parents divorced, and I moved to New York with my father. Then we were randomly paired as roommates in college. And we've been boys ever since." I stop the waiter and request the dessert menu, recalling Miya's comment in the car. "Is it too personal to ask about your boyfriend?"

"What boyfriend?"

"The one blowing up your phone."

"Not too personal at all because there's nothing to tell. He cheated. I busted him. Men are the scum of the earth." Her tight fake smile makes me chuckle. "Always fishing when they have a catch."

"Men, including your brothers and father?"

"Yes, and no. I'm a realist that knows they're players just like the rest of them. But deep down, I know my brothers are amazing men, so it gives me hope that one day I'll stop attracting men scared of commitment."

Ouch.

The waiter returns in time to switch gears. Miya asks a million questions about the dessert menu, the ingredients, the specialties, and I sit back, appreciating the sight and sounds of her.

"What about you?"

I blink my eyes, and the waiter is gone. "I didn't order."

"I ordered enough for both of us."

"What?" This woman is something special.

"I order one of just about everything. I couldn't decide. It's market research," she says with a dismissive wave of her hand. "Stop stalling and answer the question."

"I'm one of *those* men. But not the scummy variety."

"That's what they all say." She leans back, crossing her arms. "Continue. This should be interesting."

I sigh. "I'm not interested in settling down, getting married, or having kids."

"Ever?"

I shake my head. "I'm upfront with the women I date. My business has me sleeping in my airplane more than my place."

She wags her head, causing her curls to bounce.

"What? They know the score when we hook up."

"I'm sure there are some women that truly are down with hooking up. But most think they can change you. That they'll be the one to slay the dragon and claim the prize."

She's right. However, admitting it now would only make me look like her scummy ex-boyfriend.

"Since we're skipping down this gold-plated trail, who broke your heart? Your high school sweetheart dumped you before the prom? You caught your fiancé with your bestie?"

"This is a little deep for our first dinner." I reach for my water, looking around for the waiter.

"Maybe. But it will douse all of this sexual tension."

Water slips down the wrong pipe. I choke, trying to breathe and get ahold of this runaway train. I stare at Miya. "Do you always say what's running through that beautiful mind of yours?"

"No, but if we plan to spend the next two months together, it's best I know now, before you take me to another fancy restaurant, deliciously wrapped in your expensive suit, looking fucking drop-dead gorgeous with your private airplane." Her mouth tightens. "It helps to know where we stand before you start looking like my dream man, and I realize too late that you're not."

"That isn't my intent."

The light in her eyes dims, and I feel responsible because she's right.

"But it was. You just didn't know it, and now we do."

The waiter arrives, and the sting of her words hovers over the table. "Miya…"

"It's okay. I'm fine, we're fine. Do you want a little of everything?" She holds up the extra plate delivered by the waiter as if she didn't just drop a grenade between us. Her tight smile and nonstop jokes tell me there's more. But instead of making an awkward situation worse, I take the offered plate, not tasting any of it.

I like Miya, beyond physical attraction. And long after I drop her off, with a confirmed restaurant to visit Friday, I'm left wondering, how did I manage to fuck up a perfect night?

CHAPTER 9

IT'S BEST I know now… Those five words haunt me for three weeks. We've met at the same time, the same place. Each dress had me on the edge of my seat with anticipation. Miya's chipping away at my resolve to leave her intact when I walk away. That I don't ruin a budding friendship with her and a lifelong friendship with Kamal because…

I can't even say it's just my hormones. Yes, I want her body, but with every smile, every joke, and every dance break, she's taking a little more of my heart. And I can't stop it.

"Do you expect the chicken to eat itself?" I ask, hiding my laughter.

It's another Sunday, and we're closed off in Southern Soul. Miya wants to add hot wings to the menu. So tonight, instead of visiting a restaurant, I ordered wings from the top vendors in the city.

"Shut up, Dean. I can't concentrate with you breathing down my neck. Damn, give a sista some space."

The wings are spread out on the prep station. She's staring at them, scared to try them. She picked up each basket, smelling them, and her nose wrinkles on all the hot favors.

"Dean…"

"Yes, Miya."

"I hate hot stuff."

"Are you allergic?"

"Forget it." She rolls her eyes and flicks her hand.

Most of the renovations are complete. We're now at the point of working to rebuild the menu. But first, the wings.

"Are you allergic? It's a simple question," I ask again, taking a step closer.

"You need to take a nap," she mumbles, dragging a finger over the piece of chicken, and she dabs it on her tongue.

"Miya, bite it. It's not that hot. Watch." I grab one and down it, and suddenly my mouth is on fire. "*Oh, shit.*"

"See…. See, I told you that shit's too hot." She

folds over, laughing while I shove my head under the faucet.

"What did you order?" I laugh, my mouth still burning. "Those are out."

"Told you." She sticks her tongue out, and I want to sample it.

"You shouldn't do that."

The sexual tension between us is so thick it's amazing we get any work done. The only way I'm managing is by keeping her at arm's length.

We don't touch except to shake hands. We don't sit too close. Once, we tried a one-armed hug, and the moment her breast brushed my chest, we both groaned. So, yeah, touching is a no-no.

It's like we're underage instead of adults. My respect for my best friend still lingers in my mind, but even that is starting to wear thin. Not because I don't respect his wishes, but the urge to have her is growing at a rate that all I see, hear, taste, and desire is Miya.

"I'm ignoring you. Ready?" Miya walks over to the stack of index cards. She grabs a handful shuffling through the dishes.

I drag over feeling frisky today, although I've had a long week. The reward of seeing her smile at the end of a hectic week makes all the extra travel worth it.

"Let's do it in the dining room. We can spread out." I open my notes on my phone and my dictation app. Miya has a journal with her observations from each of our field trips.

I push several tables together and grab a stack of index cards.

"We have appetizers, salads, entrees, side items..."

"Plates, sandwiches, salads, sides..." she corrects.

I nod. Touring the other establishments and comparing it to the soul food restaurants has been eye-opening.

"Will you have an *a la carte* section?" I ask.

"Yeah, we have to. That provides options for people who eat different diets—vegan, vegetarian, and gluten-free dishes."

I smile. "Of course. Specialty coffee?"

"I'll have to run it by Kamal. We don't have an espresso machine. If we do, I'd want to send at least three staff members to barista training."

"Is it in your budget?"

She rolls her eyes, "No. But it won't stop me from asking."

Knowing Kamal, he'll get it even if he has to pay for it out of his pocket.

"What about bread?"

"No, not as a category. Each plate will come with cornbread and the option to substitute a roll, white or wheat bread."

I nod my approval. Streamlining will make for a

better experience. "It's time to build. No more than seven items per category."

"Seven?"

"Seven. And you don't have all night." I point to the tables. "Layout your cards."

I sit back and watch her flip through her index cards. She's a thoughtful chef, preparing each dish with care. And I expect we'll be here all night.

"I can't do this without music. I'll be right back."

She runs off, and I rest my head on my folded arms. This week I topped out at five states. Then a nonprofit in Nevada called today. I need one full weekend with nothing but my bed and Miya. I sit up taller, not sure if adding her to my list of necessities is wise. She reenters the dining room and pops her buds in her ear.

"What's up with you and your music?"

"I live by a soundtrack. It helps me think, cry, let go, etcetera. I have a song for everything." She smiles, scanning through her phone.

"Everything?" And a thought crosses my mind. "What about me?"

Her eyes round. For all of our physical precautions, nothing masks the way she looks at me.

"Is that a yes or no?"

"What are you doing, Dean?" Her eyes narrow to slits.

"I'm asking a question. Do you have a song for me? You said everything."

"I'd rather stick to the menu." Her voice is so low I almost miss it.

With an open hand, I gesture to the tables. She steps forward with a cautious eye on me. Then she presses play. The volume is loud enough to hear the cadence. Definitely Beyoncé, another one of her favorites. After a few minutes, she sings about hot sauce, and I know I'm right. Then she falls into her own world.

The journal is set aside, and she snaps and rocks from table to table, mumbling to herself. And I sit back watching the sway of her hips, reminding myself about my best friend and that damn coin toss.

"Does it have to be seven? Dean?" She removes a bud.

"Yes, seven or less. This isn't The Cheesecake Factory."

"Then I need another category." She spins around and slaps five cards on the table.

I walk over and glance over her shoulder. "What are these?"

"Miya's Weekly Picks." She looks back at me, and I could kiss her if I move a few inches closer.

I open my mouth to refute, but she jumps in.

"One of the things I noticed at each establishment they offered either a manager's special or a catch of the day. It was a physical insert or on a bulletin board. I think this would be a great way to try new features for the menu, to test recipes, or to highlight seasonal fruits, vegetables, or even holidays."

I open my mouth again, and she holds up her index finger.

"And… I'm the executive chef."

I smile. "And what's that supposed to mean?"

"What I say goes? And what Miya wants…

"Miya gets."

"I know you were a smart one." She sticks out her tongue again, and I close the space between us until the curve of her ass rests against my stomach.

Her heated gaze looks up at me. It's like they're begging me to do it.

"We're done for the night." I step back. "Take pictures of your selections, and we'll get them over to the design team to start menu mockups. Next weekend you'll prepare the full menu. I need some air."

I can't keep doing this to myself. My level of sexual frustration mixed with exhaustion has me on edge and liable to take her on the table for the world to see. And with that thought, it's time for me to take my ass home.

IT'S WEEK SIX, and we're back in the kitchen. The aroma is robust, and I'm ready to dig into every dish. I sit back, watching Miya. Today, she's listening to a slower tempo song. I can tell by her body movements. Every once in a while, she stops snapping her fingers, mumbling a few words. But we have a problem.

"Miya…" I call between repeats.

"Where are your recipes?"

She taps her temple.

I shake my head. "That won't work. We need consistent output. Same products in, same dishes out to the customers."

"Well, you'll have to take my word for it. I don't cook with recipes." Her voice hikes mirroring mine.

"You need to have them written by next weekend."

"What? You're tripping." She puts her buds back.

"Miya, this isn't negotiable. The recipes roll into the inventory, the inventory rolls into the budget, the budget rolls into the bottom line."

"And your nasty-ass attitude rolls into goodbye." She tosses the spatula. "Either you need to get laid or get some sleep. Don't take your stress out on me."

"What does me getting laid have to do with you having recipes?" I ask.

"Grouchy means you're either hungry, horny, or tired. Handle it and stop riding my ass. You never said I had to have printed recipes. Don't pop the shit up now and expect me to jump, especially with that attitude."

She storms towards the door.

"Miya, we don't have time for this. You have one week until you're presenting the menu to Kamal."

"Cook the meals your damn self. I'm done. Bye."

Stress. This isn't fucking stress. It's sexual frustration. Having her right here, walking around in fucking tights, and I can't touch her. Something's got to give, or I'm going to lose my mind.

I call Channing and tell her to cancel my appointments for tomorrow. I need a day to breathe and regroup. I head to the hotel.

After a shower, my stomach groans. As I pick up the phone to call Platinum Prestige to order dinner,

Miya crosses my mind. I took my frustration out on her, and that wasn't my intent.

I sit and call her.

"What?" She answers on the first ring.

"I'm sorry."

"You damn right, you are." The line goes dead. I stare at the phone and laugh. It's possible I love her crazy ass, and I'm too tired to fight this foreign feel occupying my body.

It could have been on sight, and I have no idea what I plan to do about it. I guess I can start by getting back in my lady's good graces. I chuckle, *my lady*, oh, she's going to blow a fuse with that one. I call her back.

"I think we accidentally got disconnected."

"Don't play with me, Dean. You have me so angry, and I'm starving after working in Dean's fucking sweatshop."

I try to hide my snicker.

"And if you laugh, Imma drop your ass in the deep fryer."

Then I burst. I laugh at the thought of Baby Miya dropping me in the deep fryer, and I'm crying.

"Baby, I'm sorry..." I howl, unable to stop. "I think you'd do it too. Man, I needed that laugh." I sniff, sitting up. "What can I get you to eat?"

"Junk food."

"Give me a couple of hours."

"I'll give you one." She hangs up on me for the second time.

Tough as fucking nails. I make a call and climb in my rental car. I drive across town, parking behind her car, and intercept the delivery guy. Then I knock on her door.

Miya opens with a hand on her hip.

I smile. "I have burgers, tacos, fries, chicken nuggets…" I push the bags around. "Strawberry milkshake, chocolate chips cookies, and there should be…" Then I spot it. "Fried cheese-stuffed jalapeños."

Miya stares at me and snatches the bags. "I could kiss you, but I'm still pissed. Come in." She turns to walk off and spins back around. "Thank you."

I follow her. This is my first time inside her place. The feel of home overtakes me. She disappears, and I take my time getting a good look around.

"Do you want something to drink?"

"Yeah, whatever you got." I see the same family picture from her phone on the fireplace. I can clearly point out all of the Montgomerys in a series of pictures, from infant shots to more recent family pictures.

They all look so happy. Skiing, on the beach, at Disney, at a park.

"Where's this one at?"

Miya trades a glass for the picture. "Oh, this was a family reunion in Raleigh. The start time on the invitation was ten, and we didn't eat until after six." She wags her head.

"And this one?" I see water in the background, and they're all squeezed into the frame.

"Saint Tropez. Come on and eat while it's hot."

She has the food spread out like a buffet. "This is kind of gross."

"Don't rain on my big girl parade. We'll eat, and then we'll find a solution to these recipes. But don't utter a word about Southern Soul until I eat."

Miya sits and does a happy wiggle extending her hands across the table. I stare, unsure what I'm supposed to do.

"Pray."

"Oh…"

She closes her eyes, and I watch her. I listen as she prays over our dinner, my lack of rest, and the menu. The words filter in and out but what stays is how her hands feel in mine. I can be honest with myself that I'm feeling Miya, everything about her from her beauty, her intellect, her sass. And at the risk of losing my life, I think it's beyond like, and knocking on the door of love.

Miya opens her eyes, and I'm still stuck on stupid.

"You can't keep looking at me like that."

"I'm trying…"

"Try harder because you're making it damn-near impossible to remember you're my brother's best friend, you're not here to stay, and I've sworn off relationships." She takes a bite of a burger. "How did you do this?"

Is that the list of barriers between us? I want to ask about her list, but I need to decide if I'm willing to risk my twenty-year relationship with Kamal.

"Platinum Prestige. It's a concierge service. They cover everything from fast food runs to booking private jets."

"How'd you remember?"

I tap my head. She told me once how she dreamed of having the best from every fast food restaurant.

"Thank you. This almost makes up for you snapping at me." She points a french fry in my direction. "So, tell me, what's got you all tied up in a grouchy knot?" She sips from her strawberry milkshake.

I blink, not sure where to start.

"We have a lot of ground to cover here. Start at the top, and I'll ask questions to fill in the gaps." She winks, and I tell her.

I cover every project on my list. The words rush out like one of her killer run-on sentences. I weave from state-to-state. As promised, she follows by asking questions, and she slows me down when I miss what she deems an important detail. Like the name of the charity. The plans for the different shelters. The amount DEK Ventures has raised to fund many of these charity projects.

"I don't know how you do it."

"Me neither. A couple are near completion. This one and New Orleans."

"What do you do for fun?"

We stand gathering the empty bags and containers. We managed to eat everything. She points to the trash can and starts cleaning the table.

"I hang with Kamal and Emmitt. We usually take a few trips a year, and I attend social engagements with clients."

"Let's sit over there. Want some coffee?"

"Yeah. What about you?"

"Cooking is my job and my hobby. I like attending concerts when I can, but most of my time has been dedicated to building my career."

"What made you choose Chicago?"

"A guy." Her flat delivery says, leave it, but curiosity makes me ask a follow-up question.

"Is that the person calling nonstop?" Her phone rings almost constantly throughout the day, but surprisingly it's quiet tonight.

"Yeah. He doesn't understand that having another woman in my bed means we don't go together anymore." She shakes her head as if flabbergasted. "I think I need to learn how to say it in another language. Spanish or something," she mumbles to herself. "Here."

I take the mug and sip. It's the way I like it.

"You act surprised. We've been together for almost six weeks. You're like clockwork. Same thing, same time, until you're grouchy, like tonight. What gives?"

I stare at her. "You."

"Me? Look, I put together the menu. I haven't been late. I followed all your little Dean*isms*."

"My what?"

"Stand like this. Cook like that. Suck it up. You can do better than this. Make the dish explode." She mimics my voice, and I laugh at her accuracy.

"I'm not that bad."

"Are you sure about that?" She snickers, looking over the rim of her cup.

"Okay, maybe I am." I lean back, relaxing a little more in her presence. This time is sexually frustrating, but I enjoy spending time with Miya. It's a highlight of my week.

"You run a tight ship because you're stretched

thin. And I get it. I also appreciate what you're doing for us."

I nod, letting her words soothe my tired soul. "What about you? You're spending all your weekends with me, you're dodging your ex, and you're taking on this new position. What do you want outside of all of this?"

"After I get rid of you?" she jokes, but our gazes lock.

"Yeah, when you rid yourself of my professional guidance."

"Oh, that's what this is called? Huh! I call it being a pain in my ass."

I laugh. "You always got jokes. But I'm going to miss hanging out with you."

"Ahhhh… Still, trying to hit me with those five-dollar come-ons? I won't miss this extra work. I'm ready to get back to just cooking."

I nod. "You've done the hard work. I'm impressed."

She smiles, curving into a stretch, and my eyes follow the rise and fall of her chest. She moans and settles back into the corner of the couch.

"I'm just doing my part to protect and build our family business. And I always want to cook in Mamma's kitchen. And now I am, thanks to *you*. But that doesn't change my question. What's going on?"

"I'm having a rough time making a decision."

"Really? Tell me, maybe I can help."

I sit my mug on the coffee table, turning my body towards her. "I'm struggling between my relationship with my best friend and an uncontrollable desire to kiss you."

I'M DREAMING. I had my junk food buffet, and now Dean's asking to kiss me. My mouth snaps shut, and I blink several times. *Did Dean just say he wants to kiss me?*

I pinch myself, then him.

"Ouch."

"So, we're not dreaming." He shakes his head, moving closer, dragging his tongue over the lips that caress me every night in my dreams. I can't close my eyes without seeing Dean, and my heart wants this more than anything.

The man looks at me, and my heart leaps out of my chest. He smiles, and I'm a babbling idiot. But the moment we turn in this menu, he's done.

The renovations are almost complete. This menu is the final piece.

"I don't think that's a good idea."

"Say yes, Miya."

"Is this a test?"

"A test?"

"Yes, Dean, a fucking test. You know I have feel-ings for you. You know I'd like nothing more than to jump your bones or have my bones pounced, or any type of bone motion would be preferred, but... Are you laughing at me?"

"Baby, I've waited over a month to kiss you, and you tell me no?"

"No, I mean, yes. Hell, you have me so fucking crazy right now. Yes, I want to kiss you, and then what, Dean?" My eyes slide to his lips, and it's a mistake.

Dean's been careful to limit our physical contact. We've held hands a few times. But for people spending time together around the clock, we've been careful about not crossing *that* line.

My cheeks are on fire, my heart drops to a rhythmic cadence in tune with the throb between my thighs. He slips his hand around my neck, coaxing me forward, and his eyes hold mine, not blinking or looking away. A slow smile builds, and I hold my breath until our mouths touch.

He doesn't move. Neither do I.

I exhale as he kisses me. I inhale, kissing him back. He pulls me closer, and the antsy unrest that started the moment we met sighs. The sounds of pleasure with each peck, moan, and nibble affirms my suspicion that Dean is a dynamic kisser.

The same passion and precision he's shown in the kitchen are applied to my mouth, and I can't get enough. His tongue strokes mine, thrusting, claiming until my exhaustion is clouded by my desire.

His lips explore, and he takes his time. Then he pulls away, and I yank him back. This time he demands more. His unmasked hunger fills my body with heat, and I spread my legs, and he settles against my body taking us back to the couch.

Our bodies rocking, mouths exploring. His kisses trail off down my neck, down my chest, brushing across my breasts. He teases my nipple through my shirt and works his way back up my body.

The length of his cock rests against me, and the moment I reach for it, Dean sits back.

The fire in his eyes tells me we're thinking the same thing. I reach for the hem of my shirt and pull it off. Before it hits the floor, the satin of my bra is pulled aside, and my nipple is in his mouth.

"Dean…"

The same hands I watch knead dough cups my ass, pressing our bodies together. I rock against the length of him. The tingle starts between my thighs, and I arch, reaching for the sweet release that oh so near. I'm standing on the edge, and the man isn't even inside me.

He slips his arms behind me. Handling my body with absolute care. Taking total possession. He sits me up, wrapping me in the strength of his arms.

My legs lock around his body. The friction of his motion is pushing me near the end. I've never had a man lift and move me without some much as a grunt. Then his tongue dives in, and I can't breathe.

"Look at me, Miya," he whispers.

I open my eyes.

This is it. The promise that every gaze deposited. The assurance that we have run long enough. I gasp, standing on the edge of completion.

His bare hand slip through the fabric of my leggings and grip my ass. His thrusts move like we're having sex, and I feel it through the thin material. My eyes roll back.

"Look at me."

"*Fuck…*"

My head falls back. I'm cussing, screaming his name. I latch on to his neck, and he groans, letting me ride the wave.

When I finally open my eyes, I see his regret.

"I gotta go." He squeezes my nose and swat at it, but I know what he's doing.

"Leave."

"What?"

"You want to leave. Leave." I move to get up, and he holds me tighter.

"You're not about to push me away."

"Dean, you just gave me the best orgasm of my life with my clothes on. But I see the regret in your eyes. You know you're way out."

"I didn't mean to…"

"Now, I know you gotta go." I push against his chest. I'm shirtless with one titty in my bra and the other out. I spot my shirt and use it to cover myself.

I point to the door because I'm too embarrassed to do anything else.

He reaches for me. "Miya…"

"Dean, if you touch me, Imma lose my shit. Just go, damn."

I walk off to my bedroom. Leave it to me to pick the wrong guy again.

The married guy. The unavailable guy. The cheating guy. Now I can add the commitment-phobe to my list.

"I'm not leaving until we talk."

"Talk to your damn self."

I woke the next morning to a note. Dean had to fly out, but my assignment is the same. He'll call at five to check-in.

"Chicken shit."

I toss the note aside. The menu is technically done. Dean emailed my pictures and his notes to the design team last night. There's no reason for him to return.

Why did I let him kiss me? And touch me?

My eyes fill with unshed tears. "No, you're fuckin' not! I'm going to finish and move my ass on."

For the record, I've done well. Over a month of working in a pressure cooker, visiting almost twenty restaurants, analyzing their menus, working on our menu, and working at Southern Soul. I'm due for a good cry. But I promised myself I won't.

"Big girls don't cry. But they can call their mammas."

I call the restaurant since I'm not on schedule until tonight. I'm so thankful she wanted to finish out the year in the kitchen. We've alternated Saturdays, and I've worked Monday through Thursday. Then she'll turn over the reigns at the end of the year if I get a majority vote. Since my siblings and I are equal owners, we require a majority vote to implement all changes. No Montgomery outweighs the other, not even Mom and Dad.

"Hey, Mamma."

"Hey, baby. How's it going?"

"It's going. Dean popped an assignment on me last night, and I'm wondering if I can get the week off. I want to finish this and prepare for the tasting Sunday. And I'll still cover the baking Saturday." I add.

"Let me check the schedule."

I walk over to my dining room table, and I recreate the layout we had last night.

We're still operating with a low kitchen staff. So, Kamal told Ebony, his publicist, to stop promoting until we're ready to publicize for the grand reopening. He and Q are using this time to train the staff and get the back office tasks complete. Once the new menu's in place, we'll hire more kitchen staff and start opening for Sunday brunch twice a month.

We thought this transition from our parents to us would take a few months. But it looks as if we'll hit a year since we started this process—from the moment Kamal returned to us officially opening on Sundays.

Kamal's led us through this process slowly and methodically with Dean's help. I push Dean and that damn note out of my mind. I'm still not sure how I plan to handle him.

However, the two decided to make the changes slowly to allow our regulars time to adjust to the differences. He changed the exterior, paved the parking lot, updated the dining area. Kamal's even opened a Sunday here and there to keep from doing too much, too soon. The last change—before announcing us at the new management—is the menu. And I expect some pushback.

The week he debuted the interior's remodeling, we received a lot of complaints from our senior citizens. But Kamal assured them Southern Soul Houston is the same. She's just getting a facelift.

"Baby, you still there?"

"Yes, ma'am."

"Take the time off. We'll work out the schedule. Todd's asking for a few extra hours anyway. What assignment are you working on? Do you need my help? Is it more recipe tasting? Because the girls and I can stop by and help."

I inherited my string of questions from Mamma. Her and the girls—Lillian and Reese—loved it when I worked on the dessert recipes. Now, their parents probably had fits because those girls were amped on sugar.

"No, ma'am. I need to write the recipes. How's it feel to have Reesie back?"

"I miss that baby something fierce. Who knew I could love her so much?"

Another hiccup in the transition was Jayda and Reese leaving Houston and returning to live in Los Angeles. We thought Kamal would stop, but he pushed through. My brother was like the walking dead. He worked around the clock. I thought he'd work himself to death, but the boys took care of him. My brothers covered the shifts since my focus has been on finishing this menu, and I'm almost there.

But a part of me wonders, what will happen next? Dean's done helping Kamal, and this is his last tether to Houston. Will we still talk? Will he visit? Will I see him again? Do I want to see him again?

My heart skips. Yes, I want to see him again. Thoughts of how he had me melting in his hands only to pull away make me wonder if that kiss was all he needed to get *us* out of his system. But it only charged me up. I didn't sleep a wink last night because he kept whispering in my ear.

"Miya, baby, are you all right?"

"Yes, no, I don't know." I sigh. "Dean is being Dean. I'm ready for all this extra work to be done, is all."

"*Hum.*"

"What's that about?" I sit on the couch.

"Nothing."

"Your nothing sounds like *something*."

"It's not. How can I help?"

"You wouldn't happen to have all your Southern Soul recipes typed and formatted in the computer so Dean will get off my ass, would you?" I'm rolling my neck as if I'm talking to Dean and not my Mamma. The man has me losing my mind.

She chuckles. "He's on your ass? That sounds… *interesting.*"

"It's not, believe me."

"You sure about that?"

I lean forward, wondering what she's hinting at. But the chicken shit in me is *not* ready for that conversation.

"Yes, ma'am."

"Well, if it's any help, I don't have them typed, and it's not all of them, but the core dishes I have them written in an old binder at the house."

"What? You do?"

"Yeah. You'll have to update them and type them."

"I'll take it." She tells me where they are at the house, and I run over to their house to get them.

By the time Dean video calls, I'm in recipe heaven. "You're a fucking genius!"

"Thank you, but what did I do?" He's sitting back with New York behind him. However, the unrest in his eyes tugs at my heart.

"Dean, do I need to come to New York?"

"No, ma'am. Not if you plan to rip me a new one. I'm too tired to fight." He laughs, but it doesn't reach his eyes. He's dressed in a white button-up with his sleeves rolled back. The ache in my chest doesn't give a damn about him backing out last night.

"You can't keep going like this. It's not healthy."

"I won't."

"Promise me you'll take care of yourself the way you take care of everyone else."

"I will." His gaze drops from mine.

"Say it like you mean it because I don't believe you for one second. Dean, say I promise…"

"I promise I'll take care of myself."

I look at the man who's managed to confiscate my heart. *God, I didn't want him to, and I have no clue what it means.* What if my brothers flip? And why didn't I feel this way about Corey, and I thought we'd get married?

Dean had me screaming his name in my clothes. I can't even imagine how I'll feel when we have sex.

Oh shit... When?

I shake my head. I'd probably go apeshit crazy over his fine ass. Some good peen will do that to the sanest woman, and I teeter toward *in*sane frequently.

"I owe you an apology," he says.

"If you want to apologize about kissing me senseless, and giving a much-needed release, keep it to yourself. I don't want it. Moving on."

I flick my hand, knowing Dean has one foot out of the door. Why complicate things? It is what it is. So, I'll leave last night where it is and focus on finishing the job in front of us. He probably has a woman on every job for all I know.

Ouch... that hurts to think about.

It's time to accept that some men aren't the forever type. I can't love him or fuck him into monogamy, and I'm not sharing. Corey made sure I learned this lesson the hard way. And I'm an excellent student. There's something about walking into your own home and seeing a naked stranger lying on your side of the bed.

But thankfully, my anger about last night disappeared the more this lesson sunk in. It will take me all week, but it will pay off in spades.

"In that case, I'm listening, babe."

It's the fourth time he's called me baby, babe, or some sort of endearment. I'm not even sure he realizes. And I only notice because my damn heart bottoms out. Again, I ignore it and continue.

"You're a genius because you held your ground. It just hit me that transcribing these recipes will help me do something I've been kicking around in my head."

"And what's that?"

"I liked how some of the restaurants had meals designated for healthier choices. Now, with the recipes, I can test ingredient substitutions. Maybe one day, we can have a specialty menu for people with health conditions like diabetes, high-blood pressure, celiac disease, or even vegan, vegetarian, pescatarian. The options are truly endless."

"I like the way you think, Chef."

"Thank you." I'm beaming. I know I am because my face is hot and my chest is full, and I've worked damn hard for this. "Will you be at the tasting?"

"Do you want me there?"

I nod, then answer, "Yes."

"Then, I'll be there."

"But Dean, not if—"

"Miya, all you have to do is say the word. And I'm there."

This man can spread my ass out on the damn table for the world to see, and I'd merely say, *yes*. And for all of my running, and all of my avoiding, I truly don't want to spend my life without him. But the renovations are complete. This menu is the final piece, and Dean has one foot outside the door.

I guess I better get over it, and him quick.

MIYA GIVES ME A FAKE SMILE, but the questions linger in her eyes. I crossed a line with her last night that I promised myself I wouldn't. I wanted to complete the job for Kamal and pursue Miya freely. But last night, I cracked, and the next thing I knew, we were kissing, and I was seconds from having all of her.

I can't talk with Kamal until Miya, and I are on the same page, so I call Emmitt knowing some fuckery is about to go down.

"Yo, what's up with you?"

"State hopping. What about you?" I ask.

"Man, they're trying to get the whole ten million out of my ass. I think I'm retiring after this. My body ain't what it used to be."

"I believe it when I see it."

He laughs. "Yeah. I think the same. But when it's my time to leave, I want to walk off the field, not get carried off."

"I feel you on that one."

I played football, but it was never my thing. My natural talent, paired with exceptional coaches, took me pro, but food was always a place for me to express myself. I think that's another reason Miya and I click. She gets it. When she loves a dish, you see it from her head to her dancing feet, swaying hips, and damn…

I'm back to Miya.

"So, what's up? I'm stuck in this ice bath."

Emmitt pulls me back, and I'm wondering where to start. So, I begin with my dilemma.

"I kissed Miya." The line goes dead silent. "E, did I lose you?"

"No. Have you lost your damn mind?"

"No, man, I love her."

"You what?"

I can see his head shaking. "I know. I tried to… fuck, I don't know what I tried to do." I rub a hand over my face searching for the words, and come up empty. All I know is the burning in my chest and the overwhelming sense of loss that hit me the moment I turned in that menu. It's unexplainable. "It just happened. Loving her just fucking happened."

Man, I got this shit bad, and I don't even know

where to begin. It's like each little moment built on the last and rolled into the next. And a part of me knows Miya had me from the moment I saw her dancing in that kitchen. It's like she latched on to my soul, and I'm not ready to let her go.

Every time I leave Miya, I'm calculating when I'll get back to her. Every time I hear her voice, I see her smile. But I'm not sure she's over her last dude or if she's interested in more. Or if I'm interested in more. And what the fuck is more?

Marriage?

Kids?

All the shit I've sworn off. And the unequivocal answer is yes. Yes, I want all of it—marriage, kids, forever—with Miya Montgomery.

I fold forward and exhale all the tension assaulting my body. That's it. I want more, and I want it with her. But does she want the same?

"Dean, wanting to fuck your best friend's sister, *never* just happens." He's quiet and mumbles, "Remind me to never get pussy in Texas."

I shake my head. "E, man, you live in Dallas."

"Oh shit, you're right."

I laugh. "Man, you might need to stop playing ball now."

We laugh.

"All jokes aside, you love her like, you're ready to

lock it down, or love her like you're in strong like because she does all the freaky shit you like."

I won't tell him that we haven't slept together, not because I'm worried about his response but that it's something I want to keep between Miya and I.

"The first one."

"*Dayum.* Y'all gonna have your boy our here running solo."

"Man, it just happened."

"What are you going to do about it?"

"Nothing until we close out this contract. And I know she has feelings for me, but she's on the fence too."

"Are you worried about Kamal jumping your ass?" He chuckles.

"Naw, man. I am more worried if she says no when I finally tell her how I really feel." I shake my head. "Are you coming down on Sunday?"

"Yeah, I'll be there. But I ain't eating shit, drinking shit, touching shit. Y'all asses dropping like fuckin' flies."

He's right. First Kamal, now me.

"You can be next."

"Oh, fuck no. I like it light and easy. Variety is the spice of life." He goes quiet for a while, then asks, "Are you happy?"

"I am. She's home and doesn't even know it."

I'm sitting in New York in my cousin's penthouse because I don't own a home. Never felt the need to since I never stay in one place long enough. But spending time with Miya let me know, my home is wherever she is.

"That shit's too deep for me. Sounds like you need a damn cigarette." He chuckles. "Save me a seat in the front row because, in love, Kamal is crazier than player Kamal."

"Man, you're a fool. The only person that can stop me is Miya."

"Do you think she'll say yes?"

"I hope so."

CHAPTER 12

How did I end up here? I shove the buds in my ears, and the magic of technology strips away the world. I'm alone with my current favorite song and my thoughts. Thoughts making sleep impossible, and insanity real, and love out of my reach.

Everything, including this kitchen, makes me think of Dean Wellington—the enemy to my attempts to remain sane and rational. This whole situation is blowing up in my face, and it's all because of him.

He's perfect, except he wants none of the things I've always wanted, which means he's imperfect. A southern gentleman to his core, door opening, and smoldering gazes that make me thank God I'm a woman.

And I know he'll be perfect for someone else, and

that hurts worse than knowing I'll probably never see him again.

Just every damn thing is all wrong.

I put my phone in airplane mode and sprinkle the surface with a generous coat of flour. Six weeks of Fridays, Saturdays, and Sundays, long nights talking about our childhood split between two households. Good wine and fantastic food while we discussed our career goals and the future. We shared everything, all while avoiding the elephant in the room.

The fact that we're carved from the same soul.

The thought slams into my chest like a wrecking ball, and I can't breathe. I grab the edge of the station to stabilize myself.

He laughs at my sarcasm. He backs off when I need time to process. He's…my soulmate. But how? Why? When he doesn't want a committed relationship, and I want marriage, and babies, and forever, and *him.*

God, how can life be so cruel? My eyes water and I can't see through my tears. I promised not to cry, but this one I can't help. How do I always find myself here? On this side of love? It's like I get all the damn heartbreak without love.

Real.

Love.

"Make the fucking bread, Miya. Damn."

I use the apron crumpled in my hands to dry my eyes, then I toss it in the hamper for the laundry. Armed with a fresh apron, it's time to act like an adult. And adulting with a crushed heart is torturous and makes me crave carbs.

I drop the prepped dough on the metal table, and it buckles under the weight of my frustration. Thanks to Dean and his excursions, my size eighteen frame is a little softer than I'd like. But homemade bread is the perfect balm for a broken heart.

So, I make the yeast rolls. The way my grandmother made them. The way my mother taught me. The way I learned right here in this kitchen when I used to beg to lick the dough because I thought it was a giant sugar cookie.

It's Saturday.

I finished the majority of the recipes. Dean submitted the revised menu. The design team created a mock design for me to share tomorrow during my little showcase. This morning, as promised, I'm at Southern Soul making the first batch of bread, biscuits, and muffins.

It's one in the morning, and I couldn't sleep. Dean called yesterday and said his plane was grounded, and like the storm disrupting life in New York, a range of emotions threaten to take me under.

The job he thought would take eight weeks, and I

demanded we shorten, took us roughly six, and now we're done.

No more weekends visiting restaurants. No more recipe tasting. No more pain in my ass demands. I should be happy, ecstatic, fucking fantastic to finally have time to myself. I had a celebratory dance in the middle of my living with the music blasting because my permanent position with Southern Soul is practically guaranteed after the showcase tomorrow. It's so freaking close. Then like a thief in the night, it hit me. Getting the job of my dreams means no more Dean, and today the bread will pay.

I knead until my shoulders ache, cutting biscuits, shaping rolls, drizzling sugary glaze over cinnamon rolls. I should have selected a better song, but the singer's groan underscores the road I've traveled to get to this weekend. This is my fucking Super Bowl, my March Madness, and I can't lose my cool over a man.

Not even Dean.

My small tasting has morphed into an event. As of this morning, the RSVPs hit over one hundred family members, friends, and all of the chefs that helped with the process of creating the new menu. I decided to embrace my inner Dean and give them an experience, starting with giving tomorrow's event an official title: *The Taste of Southern Soul.*

Dean praised my decision, and he said he would

be my right-hand man until the freak snowstorm grounded him. So, instead of sitting at home sulking, I'm here preparing what I can for our usual Saturday rush, and then I'll prep for tomorrow.

Robotic work feels good. I bake. Not stopping until the air is rich with the scent of warm butter and sweet icing. Hours later, I walk across the kitchen to remove the final pan, and my bed is calling me. But not before I taste at least one roll. I sink my teeth into the fluffy, moist goodness.

I groan. "Perfect."

A hand grips my shoulder, and I almost jump out of my skin. I spin around, startled, "Mamma, what are you doing here?"

She plucks my buds out of my ears. "It's my kitchen today. Why are *you* still here?"

"Baking bread." She glances over my shoulder and her eyes round. I turn around, inspecting my handy work. "Okay, so *maybe* I went a little overboard."

Every surface is covered. Yeast rolls, buttermilk biscuits, banana nut bread, blueberry muffins, apple cinnamon muffins, cinnamon rolls, sausage and jalapeño kolaches, and sadly there's more.

"You think?" Mamma pats the stool, and I sit, turning off the music. She removes my hair net, cupping my face. "Why don't you just tell Dean how you feel?"

"We talked, Mamma. He told me from the jump that he doesn't want to get married or have children. I respect his decision. But I'm not interested in dating for the sake of dating."

"This isn't about what Dean wants but about you being honest with yourself and him. You'll never forgive yourself if you don't at least tell him. Then let him take it from there."

"Tell him, and then what? He wants a fling, or he gives in because I want it, and then five or ten years later, he hates me because he feels trapped." I shake my head, unable to speak the words jumbled in my heart.

I remember the look in my father's eyes right before he left us. He had the look of a caged animal, and it was like my heart saw it coming before it happened. I would never want Dean to look at me like that, especially after that kiss.

"I can't. I love him too much," I whisper.

"Sometimes, it takes standing up and fighting for love."

"Fight and love shouldn't be in the same sentence."

"Maybe. But love is a magnificent creation from a perfect Creator, delivered from flawed human to flawed human. And our junk and baggage make it hard to love and be lovable."

I think about her words, knowing I'm flawed.

"That's real talk, Mamma. It's like this rejection serves as the mirror I needed to see myself. The most humbling part is realizing my past relationships failed because my expectations were unfounded. We were doomed before we started.

"It's funny how all my past heartbreaks led to this unplanned, unexpected moment. And I wouldn't change it. Not one second of it. I needed Dean's encouragement, his pushing, I needed his creativity."

I see Dean's smiling eyes through the haze of my grief, and I smile back. He did all the things. Opened doors. Listened. Showered me with compliments. Kissed my socks off.

"He even bought me a junk food buffet." My voice cracks louder than my heart.

My mother pulls me to her chest, and I let her hold me. We rock. Then I ask the question that's haunted me for the majority of my life, "Is this what happened to you and Daddy? Did regrets tear you apart?"

"Child…" She jerks as if surprised by my question. "Your Dad and I were always meant to be together. Always." I glance up, and her smile says it all. "But the deck was stacked against us. Kenneth and I were so young when we married. Then it was common for men to run the streets as long as they took care of home. That shit didn't fly with me."

"That's right! *Mamma don't take no mess.*"

We laugh.

"Then you add in five kids, owning two businesses in different states, and immaturity. Yeah…there was a lot of immaturity. And jealousy. Your father was always a looker, had women sitting in the restaurant just to see him walk through."

"Like Kamal."

"Yes, child. Those apples fell straight from the Montgomery tree." She holds me a little tighter. "We argued and fought. I threw dishes, he walked out. I'd break it off, he'd sleep in my driveway. But we had our beautiful babies to think about. And we held on, longer than we should have, or not long enough, I guess, it depends on how you look at it. It was an emotional rollercoaster until I had to draw the line."

My mind burns with the edge of familiarity in those words. Drawing the line is what got me here. That first night I built a wall with my jokes, pretending I was okay. Dean tried to talk to me, but I blocked him out. My focus was on proving myself to my family. In my head, getting it out on the table saved us unnecessary grief. But what if this is all history repeating itself? The Montgomery women fending off heartbreak by leaving first.

"What did you do?"

"I filed for divorce."

"What?"

A tear drops to the top of my head, and I sit up, switching roles with my mother, going from the comforted to the comforter—woman to woman.

"I couldn't imagine my life without him, but I knew the only way I could love Kenneth and not kill him was to let him go."

"So, you never stopped loving Daddy?"

"Never," she whispers.

"Even after the divorce?"

"Never."

"How? How did you love him and watch him with other women?" Daddy had a different woman every time we visited him. I thought he'd never settle down.

"It took the good Lord and my kids to keep me from buckling under the pressure. I had to focus on what I could control, and he had to find himself. But I guess I trusted love to bring him back to me. Then my ego got in the way, and I pushed Kenneth too far. I've lived with the heartbreak of that decision for over twenty years. So, baby, be better than your mother."

"Mamma, I didn't know." I shake my head.

"Yeah, that's probably my second biggest regret. I never wanted you guys to see your father differently, but somehow my silence made him out to be the villain of this story." She sits up, and I wipe her tear-stained cheeks with a clean portion of my apron.

"I love you, Mamma."

"Love you too, baby. Promise me you'll talk to Dean."

"How about I promise to think about it?"

"I should have named you Stubborn." She laughs, squeezing my face. "But it's your life."

"Heartbreak is for a season. But regret can last a lifetime," I deduct from my current situation with Dean and learning about my parents.

"Amen," she says.

The concern in her eyes reflects the weight of experience. However, I've spent countless days and hours with Dean. The man says what he means, and he's true to his word.

He's never fell short on a single task, never arrived late, never failed to do what he said he'd do. Therefore, I believe Dean when he said he isn't interested in a relationship.

"In a perfect world, how do you see this playing out?" Mamma asks.

"I'd be able to date Dean with the possibility of a future together. But I know it's not possible." I shrug.

"All I want at this point is to get through tomorrow and assume my position with Southern Soul. And I hope Dean can look back over our time together with fondness. Because I'll be forever grateful for what he's done for me. Either way, I'm strong. I'll be okay."

My heart tells me the road ahead will be a long one, filled with many more baking sessions. But what else can I do?

"With that said, you need to get up. You'll have a line wrapped around the building in about," I glance at my watch, "twenty-five, thirty-five, forty-five minutes." I stand, pulling Mamma to her feet.

"What is all of this?" She motions to a month's worth of bread. "I appreciate the hand, but it will take the entire city of Houston to eat all of this *damn* bread."

The laughter between us feels different. New. We shared something in this kitchen that I won't forget.

It might take me a while to move on, but I won't regret this season of my life, and I refuse to chain the weight of my romantic dreams around Dean's neck. Not after all he's done for us. And after experiencing this feeling with Dean, I won't settle.

The next guy will have to open doors, split dessert, laugh at my dry jokes, and dance to my songs on repeat. I guess I'll have to get used to my list missing one thing: *Dean Wellington*.

We walk to the sink to wash up. "Thanks, Mamma."

"You're welcome, and just in case I forgot to tell you, I'm proud of you, Miya. It feels good knowing the legacy of our food and memories are in your competent hands."

"Oh…thank you, Mamma."

"These are exciting times in the Montgomery family. Kenneth and I are remarried. Kamal has Jayda. Now all I need is more grandbabies. Lillian and Reese need cousins."

"Oh, brother. My uterus can't take it." I toss a dishtowel at her.

"What?" She dodges, pulling me back into her arms. "You know those boys will die bachelors. I doubt Rashaad will ever trust women again after Alexis. I saw that one coming, but he didn't listen to me. You're my only hope."

"Well, you might as well get used to spoiling Lillian and Reese because at the rate I'm going, you might have to settle for grand puppies from me."

She grabs her heart. "You wouldn't. Not my only daughter."

"And they wonder where I get my dramatic flair."

"Oh no, they don't wonder—they know."

We laugh and get to work finding places to store

all of the baked goods, and slowly the first shift arrives.

There's excitement in the air. Kamal returning and his work with Dean has not only transformed Southern Soul, but it's brought on a wave of new energy. I just hope they'll embrace what we've created for the new menu too.

At this point, all parties are pleased with our progress—my parents, my siblings—and it looks like we're set for launching everything at the top of the new year.

We're on the edge of greatness. I feel it.

"Planning to hang out with me today?"

"Like old times?" I ask her.

"No, like giving them a hint of what's to come." Mamma winks, and our day zooms into overdrive.

Breakfast shifts to brunch, and by the time I sit, the night staff is winding down. Mamma left a few hours ago, and I still need to prep for tomorrow.

"Miya, are you still back there?" Catrina hollers.

"Yeah, but not for long. I need to get some rest for tomorrow."

"The phone is for you."

"I got it." I grab my purse, ready to eat, shower, and sleep. "This is Chef Miya."

"Miya, we need to talk."

CHAPTER 13

I roll down the window and open my eyes. "Damn, you're beautiful."

"Now I know you're lying. But I'll take it." Miya's tired smile spreads across her face, and I know I made the right decision. "Are you trying to go to jail? You know I have nosy neighbors. They'll think I have a white man stalking me."

"They know what time it is. We need to talk."

Miya leans against the door. "Right now, in my driveway?"

"No, inside." I pinch her nose, knowing she hates it.

"Quit—you know I hate that." She smacks my hand.

I laugh, stepping out of the car. I stretch out the

hours of driving from my muscles, groaning until I feel slightly human. Then I follow her.

"Come on, you sound like an ole broke down lion."

I shake my head. Always cracking jokes. Once inside, I drop to the couch. "Man, this feels amazing."

"It's good to see you, but you look the way I feel."

The couch shifts and I open my eyes. I run a finger down her soft cheek. "And how's that?"

"Like crap."

"Well, damn, woman."

She chuckles. "You asked. So, what's up? How'd you get here? Did the storm die down?"

"Do you always have to ask a million questions at once? And you'd know the answers if you answered your phone." She pulls it out and drops her head from my sight. "Anything could have happened."

"My bad I worked in the kitchen today. But you look fine to me." She wiggles her eyebrow suggestively, still cutting up.

I put a finger beneath her chin, turning her beautiful face toward me. My contract with Southern Soul ended the moment I emailed the menu. It took driving almost twenty-four hours to realize I'm losing her. And I can't let that happen.

"Talk to me."

"Not with you looking like death warmed over *twice*." Her nose crinkles. "And I can't believe you're wearing jeans. I thought you slept in suits."

"Do I have to beg to hear about your day?"

"No, you know I love talking but—"

"Then talk. Damn."

"Three damns. Oh, this is going to be good."

I laugh until my side aches, and all the stress of getting here leaves my body. Miya, with all her extra ways, is like medicine for my soul.

Her eyes soften. "I knew you had it in you."

Spending so much time together put our friendship on steroids. Our chemistry is natural, but I've had to patiently peel this woman back layer by layer. And man, have I been on the journey of understanding her and myself.

"I'm listening." I drop my head back against the plush couch and close my eyes, waiting for the sound of her voice.

"You called about the plane, and my head went crazy. Thinking about tomorrow. Wondering if I could do it on my own...if I should share the menu with Mamma. Kamal approved it, but what if..."

"What were you listening to?" And when she doesn't respond, I open my eyes.

"Music. So, instead of tossing and turning, I went to the kitchen and baked for hours."

"Play the song for me."

"Dean." She sighs. "I'm not playing it now. It has nothing to do with this conversation. How can you ask me to tell you about my day and then switch gears?"

"What was it?" I pull out my cellphone, and she snatches it.

"Fine. You're a pain in my ass. You know that?" she mumbles, giving my phone back, and then finds the song in her playlist. "Here. I'm going to take a shower. Figure out what you want to eat. I'll be back."

I watch her ass sashay out of the room. I've had to unpack her the way I research and dissect information about a restaurant. The truth is hidden in the details. Her jokes are her first line of defense. But to get to the meaning without taking the scenic route, listen to her playlist.

Miya can listen to one song on repeat for hours. She joked about it once, and it wasn't until a couple of weeks ago that I saw the meaning of this gem of a detail. The essence of the song communicates what she's processing. Sort of like Bumble Bee in *Transformers*.

She talks through music. Her song selection is like an emotional barometer. So, instead of dragging out the details, listen to her current favorite song.

The sound of the shower fills the room, and to keep from thinking about her body covered in bubbles or about how much I'd love to join her, I press play.

A few bars in, and I'm tense. I suck in a quick breath, and my eyes bounce between the phone and the doorway. The words, the voice, the vibe tell of falling under the weight of love, waiting for the right time to learn if the feelings are reciprocated.

I sit forward, wide awake, heart racing with her red cellphone anchored in my shaking hands.

I'm drowning, and every time I think I have it figured out, I'm pushed back underwater, with my lungs demanding air, screaming for relief. The relief I only feel when I'm with Miya.

My talk with Emmitt helped uncover my true feelings. However, I can't help but wonder whether I'm the man she wants, the man she needs. But from the moment I saw her dancing around in the Southern Soul kitchen, my heart was hers. I just didn't want to admit it because I didn't believe it. How did I live thirty-three years avoiding love only for it to find me and take me hostage?

I never wanted a woman like I want her, and twelve hours into my drive, the answer crystallized. I never wanted a relationship because it wasn't Miya.

It's not about the word or a general feeling—it's about *her*.

My body stiffens, muscles rigid, heart pounding as my head reminds me of all the times I said I'd never fall in love. And now here I am, in love like a *muthafucker*.

Will she believe I want more? Will she believe I want her more than anything I've wanted my entire life?

"Dean, how did you get here?"

I'm on my feet, disoriented, yet sure.

"What's the matter? Are you sure you're okay? You're not getting sick, are you? Because I need you to make this happen. Just the list of all the stuff we have to do tomorrow is enough to make my head explode." And in true Miya fashion, she rattles along until she's sitting again, and I lower to the couch beside her.

"Does your brain ever stop?" I ask, knowing the answer.

"No. It's just my brain is…" She opens and closes her hands in a talking motion. "But I feel better with you here." She sighs, dropping her hands in her lap with a serene look on her face. "Are you ready to tell me what this is all about?"

I swallow, hoping it's not too late. "I'm thinking about how to have this conversation with you, anticipating all the way to convince you to say yes."

"Yes."

"I haven't asked yet." I chuckle. *This woman.*

"I trust you. And you're never this antsy. Both of us can't be nervous. Besides," she wags her finger in the air, "I have bullshit insurance."

"You already said yes, but what's your bullshit insurance?"

"Four big ass brothers."

I stare at her, and she bursts into laughter. I sit forward, inhaling her delicious smell, and I know this is the right move.

"I want you to be my wife. Will you marry me?"

"WHAT?" My world spins. Then the doorbell rings, and I'm somewhere in the clouds.

"I'll get it," he says, with a quick kiss.

"No, we need to talk. You don't just blurt out—"

"It's food…"

"Why didn't you say so?" I watch him walk away, certain I'm losing it. Did he just ask me to marry him? I stick a finger in my ear and roll it around. I pinch my thigh. "Ouch."

My ears are working fine, and I'm awake.

Dean goes to the door, and I head to the kitchen.

I wipe down the table and snag a few condiments from the refrigerator. Then he walks in with at least thirty fast food bags.

"Yay, junk food buffet." I catch a bag before it hits the floor. "I want you to know you have my hips spreading with all of this eating out."

"I'm cool with that. I love your thighs." I watch him open and close bags, pulling the platter to the center of the table. "And your ass—I could watch you walk away a billion times a day and not get enough of it."

He *loves* my thighs and my ass. I store that away for later too.

We work together, removing burgers and tacos and French fries until we have a thick girl's fast-food fantasy spread across the table.

"I need to sign up with Platinum Prestige because their delivery team is the bomb."

"Told you." He winks and heads to the kitchen to wash his hands.

I thought we had a big fucking elephant in the room before, but this takes the cake. I want to ask, but I want time to process, and I'm hungry. I walk over and open my mouth, but then he kisses me. It feels different, more intimate, depositing a promise in my soul that I intend to examine. I consider the perfect song to pair with it when he reenters the dining room.

"Dean, did you really just ask me to marry you?"

"Yes, Miya, I did."

I search his eyes, not sure how to take this. "Are you playing around? Joking?"

"No, I'm not. I want you to know where I stand before we see your family tomorrow."

"Okay."

It's all I got. Because my brain is spinning, and there's a table full of carbs to help me make sense of this whole situation.

We sit, and after I bless the food, we dig in, eating in silence. I open the straws and pop them into our drinks. I keep hearing his proposal in my mind, and he's moving on as if he said nothing.

"How do you feel about tomorrow?"

I shrug. "Excited and nervous. Ready to get it over with."

"That's good. It means you care." He glances at his watch, and I notice the time. I've been up over twenty-four hours.

"Did you check into your hotel?"

"Not yet, I wanted to check in with you first." He yawns, and I notice his eyes are red with exhaustion. He stands to gather our trash.

"When's the last time you slept?"

"Are you done with that cup?" He holds out a hand. I pass it to him.

"Wait, Dean." I hold up a hand. "Sit down."

Dean has a way of avoiding questions, and my tendency to ramble gives him an easy out. I think back over everything and realize he never said how he got here.

"How'd you get here?"

"I drove."

"No shit, Sherlock. The car is parked in the driveway. I mean to Houston. Were you cleared for flying?"

"No."

I'm on my pace processing without music. "I'm too tired to play a hundred questions with you, Dean. You pop up and say, oh hey, want you to be my wife. Like that shit is this normal part of our conversations."

"I drove," he says again.

I stop pacing and stare at him. He was in New York for a few days, then he was flying here for the weekend. "Wait, you're serious?"

He stands up again, walking over to the trash can. "I could have waited until I cleared the state, but by then, I was rolling."

"You drove from New York? Dean, you drove from New York. What? That's crazy. Why?"

"Because I couldn't fly in a snowstorm."

"But, it's perfectly sane to drive in one." I throw my hands up in the air. Leave it to him to make it seem like it was a walk across the street. "Why, Dean?"

"Because I told you I'd be here."

"But that doesn't mean drive." A low-grade panic is rioting through my body. "How long did it take you?"

"That's not important, Miya."

He makes another trip to the trash can, and I head to the living room to get my phone.

"What are you doing?"

"Getting answers. My brain is mush, and you want to play hide the pickle."

"What's hide the pickle?" He laughs, trying to take my phone.

I spin around, using my back to block his attempts while typing "New York" into Google Maps. The number staring back at me sucks the air out of my lungs. "You drove seventeen hundred miles."

"Yes."

The hairs on the back of my neck stand up, and I stare at him, baffled. Dean moves to take another round of bags to the trash when I stop him.

"When's the last time you slept?"

"About thirty-six hours ago."

"Thirty-six hours? Go get your bags."

He opens his mouth, and the stare I give Dean dares him to challenge me.

He returns, and I'm too pissed to look at him. "The guest room is down the hall on the left. The shower is across the hall. You should find everything you need in the linen closet behind the door."

He drags down the hall, and I don't blame him. He drove twenty-four hours, and my only question is why. Why did he do it? And is that why if felt the need to toss out, oh and I want you to be my wife?

I turn out the lights, popping my buds in my ears, hoping to make sense of Dean's change of heart and to quiet my need to bake.

CHAPTER 14

I STEP out of Miya's shower, and my eyelids weigh a ton. The strain of the trip, Miya, and overall exhaustion is on my shoulders. I throw on a pair of boxers, focused on putting one foot in front of the other.

The hallways are dark except for a light at the end of the hall. I drop my stuff in the bedroom and follow the glow. I knock on the door, and Miya removes a bud from her ear.

"How was your shower?"

"Amazing. What time are we leaving in the morning?"

"Eight."

"That sounds good. 'Night, Miya." I turn to leave because it will take the last ounce of energy in my body to make it to my room. I shake my head. That's the last time I'll take an impromptu road trip. But I did make good time.

"Dean."

I glance back.

"Why did you ask me to marry you?"

"Because I know from the moment I saw you dancing around in the kitchen that you were mine." I smile over at her, but she's not smiling. "Baby, whatever you're thinking, let's address it later. You need to rest. You have a big day tomorrow."

"Okay."

Okay, in Miya code means the shit's about to hit the fan. I lean against the doorjamb, sliding until I'm sitting on the floor. My head drops back, and I close my eyes.

"This is like that kiss," she whispers more to herself than me.

My eyes snap open. "What does that mean?"

"It means I know how you feel, and you know how I feel. You don't want to marry me, or anyone else. You said so yourself. You're not interested in commitment, and I'm not looking for a fuck buddy."

"A fuck buddy?"

"Yes, we shouldn't have crossed that line, and I'm certain you'll feel the same way after you rest."

"A nap is supposed to make me change my mind about how I feel about you?"

"Exhaustion did."

Miya throws words like sharp knives, hitting her intended target. I push up to my feet.

"I'm not doing this with you. You're right—I'm exhausted. But not enough to play this game with you tonight. Good night."

I turn to leave with adrenaline pumping through my veins. And anger sends me back, "You never asked why. Why I was against marriage and commitment? Why I didn't like playing these games? You're so caught up in your own world, in your own head, that all you think about is yourself. I'm out of here. Bye, Miya."

I walk down the hall, set on packing my bag and leaving. Women think they own the license to pain. Men go through shit too. But I choose not to walk around wearing it like a badge of honor. I sit on the edge of the bed and fall back.

This is why I stayed away from relationships. This is why… The light down the hall turns off, and I wait to hear her moving around. The sound of her tossing and turning echoes through the house, and then the house falls silent.

I'm going to take a nap and then head home. But I'm certainly not driving again. I'll have to get the jet.

I wait, hoping sleep takes me, but it doesn't. The last thing Miya needs is to sit in that bed, replaying the conversation over and over. I can't change her mind, that's not my place, but I can give her insight.

I kick my legs over the side of the bed.

"Mind if I join you?"

I turn on the lamp and see Miya waiting outside the door, her face closed as if expecting the worst. Then I notice the brown fuzzy contraption she's wearing.

"What are you wearing?"

She spins around and wiggles a long doggy tail. "It was a gift from my cousin, Quanie."

I chuckle, patting the bed beside me. I turn out the light, expecting her to sit on the other side. But to my surprise, she crawls close, lying on her side facing me. I stare at the ceiling, letting the energy of this woman seep into my pores.

My work has taught me the passion of creatives. Color, taste, texture, drama. Thriving off the element of surprise. Finding ways to make the familiar unique. But is that how I want to live my life? Not knowing whether she's hot or cold, loving or moody, with me or against me? How do I want tonight to play out?

"What are all of the decisions that led to this moment?"

I heavy sigh escapes. "Miya..."

"Dean... You stormed in, dropped a bomb, and I'm on the fucking edge of my sanity. I push because

I don't want this shit to blow up in my face. I push because it's what I do, and I don't want to do it with you. But it's harder than I thought. Plus, it seems I'm kind of good at it."

"You figured all of that in ten minutes." I turn, searching for the copper in her eyes through the darkness.

"Yeah, that and I've decided you'll have to run for the hills first."

"Really?" I trace a finger down her cheek. I don't need a light to see the fear lingering in her eyes.

"Dean..."

"How do you always smell edible?" I ask, trying to decide if that's cinnamon I smell.

"I think there's something lodged in your nose." She leans over and kisses the tip. "I've wondered about your parents and how you adjusted to their divorce? How it felt to be an only child bouncing back and forth for all those years? How you found food or whether food found you? What motivates you to fly nonstop to help others build their dreams? What you fear most? What you love more? But really whether..."

"Whether what, Miya?"

"Whether you see us when you line up the expectations you have for your life." There's a quality to her voice I've never heard before that makes me want to wrap her in my arms and protect her from the world.

"Sounds like you're fishing for secrets to sell to a rival."

"Nah, just fishing for the secrets to your heart."

"It's already yours." I kiss her, trying to find my way to her soul. A woman who makes me hot and cold, pisses me off, yet makes me feel seen and heard. Life with passion, a dash of crazy, and more of Miya is how I see my future.

I fall back. My family dynamic is nothing like hers. "You sure you want to hear all of this, now?"

"Yes, please." She kisses me, pulling back to stare into my eyes. "Everything."

"My family dynamic is nothing like yours. My Pops traveled the world and still does, representing our family restaurants, hosting culinary contests. And many days and nights, the only time I saw him was on TV." I think back and add. "He's a great father when he's around, but his ambition monopolizes all of his time."

"What about your mother?"

"She split when she realized Pops wasn't a one-woman kind of man. She sees me as a package deal with him. So, I visited her every other holiday, every other year. I guess I stopped going when I was about sixteen. Dad sent me to boarding school after I outgrew nannies." I chuckle, loving the feel of her skin beneath my hand.

"What did you do? That sounds like a story."

"I used to have sex with my nannies."

She pops up. "You what?"

"I was a horny, rich teenager. Pops came home early one day and caught me." I laugh. "I was honestly trying to get his attention. But I never stood a chance against his dreams."

"And your mom?"

"She's remarried with a family. I'm an outsider looking in on their perfect life. The life I always wanted." I trail off in thought. Mother gives her other kids what I always wanted. They get the TV mom. I get a woman who sees me through the lens of a past mistake. "That's why I always found your family fascinating."

"Fascinating?" Us?"

"Yes, seeing Kenneth and Miss Jackie showed me adults who cared about their children."

"It wasn't perfect."

"Yeah, but you never had doubts."

She shakes her head. "I guess not, but there was always this void."

"How different is it now that your folks are married again?"

"They're happy, but we're all still adjusting, some

better than others. Do you think your father will get married again?"

"Nah. He married my mom because she was pregnant." I stare at the ceiling, thinking about my life and my decisions. "I work hard like my father. But until I met you, I didn't realize I was going down that same road."

"What road is that?"

I shrug. "Loneliness. He can sleep with a different woman in every city, but he doesn't have what I see in your father's eyes when he looks at your mother." I look over at her. "I bet having Southern Soul, and five kids helped your folks come back together. My parents only had me, so once I graduated from college, that was pretty much it. Which connects to the other question about what motivates me to help others—your family inspired me."

"How?" She rolls over to her stomach.

"One Thanksgiving, my parents got their plans crossed. Mom thought I was going to Dad's. Pops thought I was going to Mom's. Both had plans without me. Your mom insisted that Kamal bring me home." I laugh, remembering my shock. "I saw your father sitting at the table and was prepared to see food flying, nasty words, attitudes. But it was the exact opposite. We pushed all the tables together and had a big family dinner. I've been chasing that feeling ever since."

I wrap an arm around her and pull her close. "I want that with you, Miya, without the divorce, of course."

"Of course… Dean, I want nothing more than to have this with you, but I don't want you to get a year or two down this road and resent your decision."

"Nah, not going to happen." I crawl over her until she's underneath me. "What I'd regret is walking away and not having you in my life? And that's a regret I don't want to live with."

I kiss her. Then roll back to my spot.

"I wish I could remember more of you from then. But my brothers had so many friends."

I kiss her again. "Let's address the last question for tonight. Can I see us in the future? You took a piece of my heart from the moment I saw you. Now, it's time for you to decide what you plan to do about it. Whether we're going to work together to give us a shot."

"I'm scared," she whispers.

"You're not the only one." It feels good to get it off my chest.

"What made you change your mind?"

"I like the scent of cinnamon."

Her laughter echoes off the wall. "Those five-dollar come-ons are strong."

"Ah, man…I remember that day. You were as tough as nails. All sass and attitude. But what sticks with me the most was your dancing."

"Bullshit!"

"All I saw was your ass bouncing around and…" I use my hands to make a cupping motion, and she struggles to stop me.

"Perv! Have you been staring at my ass the entire time?"

"Yeah. I can't help it." My laughter dies down, and I sigh. "You got a beautiful ass, babe."

"I let you dodge enough."

"I thought you'd forget." I turn, and we're nose to nose.

"Not a chance. What made you change your mind? And what if you change it back?"

"I saw you in that kitchen dancing around and—"

"Dean, you better not mention my ass."

"I'm not. Well, not now." I kiss her softly and prop up on my elbow. "You were dancing, and I couldn't remember the last time I danced just to dance. Or when I was so happy that I couldn't contain it. That's how you make me feel. Not tonight…"

"My bad."

"But the thought of getting back to you. Talking to you. Seeing you. Hearing you rattle along about your day. It makes my soul dance."

"Dean…"

"It took driving to help me come to terms with my feelings about my parents and my resulting beliefs about marriage. I won't change overnight, but I see it clearer. And I won't change my mind because I want you, Miya, all of you, even the crazy parts." She punches me on the shoulder, and I fall back, taking her with me. "I'm sure the ride won't be easy. But something in me believes we're worth it."

Miya kisses me, and I'm not drowning anymore. She runs her smooth hands up my chest, cupping my face. I snake my arm around her, pulling her against me.

Her sweet little hand caresses my rock-hard cock, and I bring her hand to my lips. "I want to make love to you. But after you have time to think about what we've said tonight."

"I appreciate that. Mind if I sleep in here with you tonight?"

"Not at all."

It seems surreal to realize that I'm not lonely anymore. That my life won't center around my career or clients. "Damn…"

"What?"

"I have a girlfriend."

"So, uh…lover boy, can we keep this between us? It's new, and my brothers are loco when it comes to me." She laughs, and I wish I could bottle it up and take it with me, so, instead, I hold it in my heart, next to her smile and her kisses.

I'll give her the time she needs, and then I'll break it to the Montgomery men. It won't be all at once. I'm much too smart to do that. But as long as I have her, I'm good.

"Babe…"

"Hum…"

"I have a song to add to your playlist."

"You do? What's it called?" " She props up on her elbow, reaching for her phone.

"I got it. It's called *One Thing Missing*."

I press play and turn up the volume. This is the song I've played on repeat for days while I tried to see my way clear to a decision. I see why she likes it. The loop of the song makes the world fade, and all I thought about was her.

By the time the song hits repeat, Miya's mush in my arms. And now I see why they call her Baby Miya. I gather my love to my chest, holding her tight, and within seconds. I'm having the best sleep of my life with my missing piece.

My Miya.

CHAPTER 15

THE MORNING SUN creeps through the blinds. Today is *The Taste of Southern Soul,* and an unexplainable calm settles over me. It feels like I've worked my entire career for this moment, but this is only the beginning. Either way, I'm about to give them a taste of what to expect when I'm the permanent executive chef.

"He sleeps," I whisper, glancing at the beautiful man beside me. Now, this is something I could get used to. I thought I knew what I was getting into with this transition, but I couldn't have planned this, and I didn't see *him* coming. And I'm pretty sure I'm engaged.

I shake my head. We talked until I could barely keep my eyes open, and although a part of me is scared to try this love thing again, I can't give in to my fears. Not if it means no more Dean.

He'll have to run first, but his character has shown him trustworthy. He's come every time I've called. The man drove twenty hours for me. That alone is enough to give him some. And last night, that song was everything, and I'm adding it to my rotation.

I slip out of bed to handle my morning business, making a pitstop in the kitchen to start the coffee. Dean and I have so much to discuss, but first, I have to secure the bag. I pop my buds in my ears to wake up my soul.

The printouts of the menu arrive via email this morning. I send them to my home office and review the design making a few minor notes. I check the RSVPs once more.

I dial my brother. "Yo, Q."

"What's up?" His groggy voice tells me he's still asleep.

"We have one hundred and fifteen people coming today."

"Word?"

"Yeah, did you hire enough staff?"

"You cook, I got the staff. Now, I'm going back to sleep. Love you."

"Love you too." I chuckle, but he's already gone.

Kamal gave us designated areas. Q is using his experience from the club and handling the wait staff and the floor. Rashaad is Kamal's second, handling the property concerns. Demetrius is a floater. He's not a front floor kind of person, but he handles the tech. The website updates, and he'll be the liaison between the design team in the future.

Today's not the official grand reopening or the pass off, but it feels like it to me. This will be the first time everyone sees the fruit of my labor. Two months of visiting, eating, testing, and now I'll reveal the official Southern Soul Houston menu.

I dance my way through the house to my closet and pull out my new chef's jacket from my brothers. They made me promise to wait until this morning to open it. I unzip the garment bag, and to my surprise, I see a custom royal purple jacket with my name embroidered on the front with the new Southern Soul logo. I open my mouth to squeal and remember I'm not alone. So, I dirty wind around until I can't breathe.

Drake and Rihanna tell me to work, and I'm about to do the damn thing!

I hold the jacket up and dance in the mirror, rocking out into my bedroom. That's when I turn around and see Dean, shirtless in his boxers. He has the hard, muscled body of a football player. And the definition in his abs is sickening.

And he's all mine…

I hang my jacket on the door and walk him to my bed, tossing my phone and headphones aside. He leans back on his elbows, watching as I remove my fluffy pajamas, kicking them aside.

"Sexy, huh?" I tease.

"You'll hear no complaints from me."

"Good, because I recall you saying you love my thighs…"

"And your ass." He sits forward, gripping my hips, turning me around. I wiggle again, this time without the doggy tail.

Dean kisses one cheek, then the other, dropping my sexy boy shorts to the floor. A trail of moist kisses starts at the base of my spine and move up. Each one etching out the world. Anticipation builds as his hands explore my waist, my stomach, cupping my breasts. And I'm eagerly waiting to touch him.

"Dean…hurry…"

"Patience, baby…" is all I hear when his hand rids my hip and travels lower, cupping my heat. He rubs my clit, and I sigh the moment the tips of his fingers part the lips and enter my dormant body.

It's been months because I refused to sleep with Corey when I suspected he was cheating. A part of me felt guilty, wondered if I drove him to have that woman in my bed. But it's neither. He made his bed, and if he hadn't, I wouldn't be here with Dean.

"I've dreamed of this, of having you, all of you," Dean whispers across my shoulder until our mouths collide, tongues teasing, as his fingers stroke me, igniting my need.

I'm glad we waited, waited for this to be more than sex. It's the beginning of something new. I pull the top of his hair, wanting more when the hardness of his cock presses against me. I push the fabric of his boxers aside, throwing my ass back until his dick slides between my cheeks. I drag my body over his loving the way he groans.

Dean holds my breast tighter, stroking my pussy faster, coaxing me to the edge of ecstasy.

"This is just the beginning," he whispers in my ear before the magic of his hands has me screaming his name. "I like the sound of that baby. I want to hear it again."

"I'm down. Do you have protection?" I ask, turning around, wrapping my arms around his neck.

He lifts me, laying us back on the bed. "I want you, but I'm willing to take our time."

"Oh no, you don't. I want all of *D* now." I grab him, and he pulls out of my reach.

"I might have one in my bag."

"And I might have one in the bathroom," I offer, loving the look of desire in his eyes for me.

"I'll meet you back in one minute."

I giggle. "The first one back is on the menu for breakfast."

"Be prepared—I fight dirty." Dean laughs.

"Talk dirty to me." I smack his tight ass. "One…two…"

"Three."

Dean is off, and I'm rolling. Then I remember I want to win. I run to the bathroom, digging around for condoms. I find two, and I stop in the bathroom doorway, watching as he spots me.

The same eyes I saw in the kitchen two months ago explore my body freely. I've never felt more wanted and desired as he licks his lips. He leans against the doorjamb with his legs crossed at the ankles.

"This is a race," I remind him.

"I know."

I freeze, seeing what he's packing in the light of day. His thick shaft flexes, making my mouth water.

"Turn on some music."

This man wants me to walk. Then the perfect song comes to mind. I glance back, ready to make this worth the wait, worth the indecision, worth staying. And I know I can't fuck a man into staying, but that won't stop me from trying.

I connect my phone to the wireless speaker and crank it up, *Sex With You*. This is when all those high-heel dance classes come in handy. I rock my body to the music, drop in a split, and roll-up. Holding his passion-filled gaze.

I throw my whole size eighteen around, then crawl across the bed with my ass in the air.

I look back.

Dean walks over, and the heat in his eyes makes my pussy jump in anticipation. His hands caress my body, up my back, he holds my shoulders, pressing my body across his rock hard dick. Then he flips me over.

Shyte...

"Is this what you've been listening to?" His hand runs over my body, dragging me to the edge of the bed.

"You have a problem with it?"

He kneels in front of me, dropping the condom he found on the nightstand. I add my two, watching him, curious about what he'll do next.

"Nope. Because every time you hear this song, you'll think about me feasting on you."

He picks up one foot, kissing my ankle. The

feather-light kisses are torture, as he whispers across my skin until his mouth aligns with my core.

"Baby..."

"Dean...you will not talk. Not right now."

"Are you sure? Because I might have a few things, you would like to hear. Actually, I'm finding the words of this song quite inspiring." He swipes between my folds with his tongue, and I'm so wet that I should be embarrassed, but I'm not.

"Like what?"

"Do you want to hear my proposal? Yes or no."

His thick tongue dips inside, and I groan. And I'm a hot second from being him to shut up and fuck me.

Damn.

My leg is dangling down his back with my pussy in his face, and this man is trying to hold a conversation. I manage to sit up. "How is it that you're mute seventy-five percent of the time, and now you want to talk?"

"Because this is a negotiation."

"No, you're taking off I have to offer today. Then his fingers play, and my hips rock to keep up.

"What are we negotiating for?" I manage before his fingers enter me again.

"*Forever.*"

Dean's doing something with his tongue, and it

has me crawling up the bed, but his strong hands lock me in place. I beg, he delivers. He commands, I obey. I die a thousand times, and he's not done.

I can't do shit but take it. And when release snakes up my spine, I buck riding his face. We play and tickle until we've almost had our fill.

Dean's unshaved face hovers over mine, and I'm glad he didn't give up on me. He grabs the protection from the nightstand.

"Are you with me, Miya? And before you answer, I'm yours, exclusively. No more games. No more hiding. It's you and me."

"I'm not asking for promises."

"But you're asking for a commitment, and I'm giving it to you with my heart."

"Then I'm all yours."

We put on the condom together, and he settles between my thighs.

I COAT myself in her wetness, teasing open her folds. Miya rotates her hips, trying to coax me inside. She's passionate and playful in bed. I never thought I'd be excited about commitment, about giving myself to one woman, but I am.

I enter her. We gasp in unison. She's deliciously

tight, holding me captive between her thick thighs. I push until I fill her.

"*Gotdamn...you...*"

"Oh, you like that?" I ask.

"Yes..."

The dance starts. I wrap her legs higher up my back to fill every inch of her sweet pussy. Her moans of pleasure drive me to whisper all the ways I plan to love her. Reminding her that this is only the beginning. Claiming her body as mine, and mine alone.

Her muscle grips me tighter. Rocking to the melody of the music. My heart pounds as I drive into her. Telling her of my love and how she's my fucking world.

"I'm about to..." she cries.

"Not without me."

I flip her over, and she sighs. "*Muthafucka....*"

I enter her from the back, and she's eating the comforter. Mumbling shit and still throwing all that ass on my dick.

"Dean..."

"Baby...*fuck*..."

She presses closer, and I increase the tempo. Slapping underscores the repeat of the song. She'll never forget this moment. Every time she hears this song, her panties will be drenched, and her pussy will beg for me.

Then she tilts her ass higher.

"Shit…"

No more words, only the sounds of her passionate cries. Her pussy grips me so tight my groans of pleasure drown out the music.

There's no turning back. I wrap my hands around her waist, pulling her to me until I tongue her down. Then we drop to the bed. I feel her heart beating against my chest. I'm worn out but not sleepy.

She stops the song, and our pants fill the room.

"Alright then…" she jokes, and I smack a kiss on her forehead.

Our laughter dies, and suddenly I want to know everything there is to know about Miya Montgomery. "Tell me something I don't know."

"Like what?"

"What's something you've always wanted outside of your career?"

"That's easy, and not to freak you out. But a family." She looks back. "I thought about what you said last night. And I guess it's probably close to how you felt alone being the only child. I used to feel that way in a house full of people. But it's because our lives were centered on Southern Soul."

She leans against me.

"That's why I'm glad Kamal is running the place. When I start my family, I want to cook and go home.

We didn't have that luxury as kids. My mother worked from open to close because it was our only source of income. Dad helped. But she and Kamal handled our daily lives."

"I guess my life was similar, except I was home alone. That's how I found sports and my friends." I kiss her shoulder. "When you say, family… A kid or two?"

She looks back again, holding my gaze.

"What?"

"You're asking me about kids."

"I am."

"I'm open but more than one." She rolls over. "You're really serious."

"I am." I glance over at the clock. I sit up, and she pulls me back. "We need to get going. You have an event to cook for."

She exhales. I want her to get used to the idea that I'm here to stay. I've never given children much consideration because I wouldn't have them out of wedlock. But since Kamal met Jayda, I've enjoyed being Uncle Dean to Reese.

The idea of a sassy little girl with Miya's sass and my eyes makes me roll her over until I'm settled between her legs again.

"Today's a big day. Are you nervous?"

"No, not yet. It might hit me once we get there."

"Then let's get moving."

"I love you, Dean."

My heart stops. I cup her face and kiss her. "I love you too. How'd I get so lucky?"

"I was thinking the same thing." She wiggles until I'm aligned and ready for another round. "Do you think we can do that again before we leave? You know, to take the edge off."

I chuckle. "I think I can handle that."

CHAPTER 16

WE ENTER SOUTHERN SOUL, and we head straight to the kitchen. Miya crosses inside in the zone, and I fall back. This is her day and her kitchen. She's done the work.

"It's game day, baby."

I smack her ass, and she rolls her eyes. "You can't do that here."

"You can demand a repeat, and I can't smack *my* ass?" I rub my body against hers.

"No, not with my brother here." She wiggles out of my grip. "Don't give me that look. You know Kamal and his damn rules."

"You're grown, and Kamal's my boy, but I don't want to hide how I feel about you."

"Just let me get through this day. Okay?" She

snuggles closer, kissing me, then she slips me a little tongue. "Set up your station."

"Yes, Chef." I glance towards Kamal's office. During the construction, we added his office and one for Miya right off of the kitchen. "I'll be back."

"Dean… Dean…" She tugs on my arms.

I stop. "Miya, as your man, you gotta trust me. I want nothing but the best for you, and after finally having you, I'm not hiding how I feel. Now kiss me, and pray we don't tear this restaurant up after I worked so hard to renovate it."

"I trust you." But I see the concern in her eyes.

"Get to work, and I'll be back."

She nods, and I smack her ass for good luck.

"Perv."

"You know it." I kiss her and head out to find Kamal.

I walk through the restaurant that's occupied the majority of my time for months. But instead of thinking about the materials, the blueprints, and the contractors, I think about how to tell my best friend I'm in love with his sister. And it's not about fear, I fear no man, but respect. Because his family is my family, and his sister will one day be my wife. It could be tomorrow, or next month, or next year. The details at this point are a mere technicality.

I enter his office, and he glances up from a document. A smile spreads across his face.

"I bet you thought we'd never get here." Kamal stands up, sitting the papers aside. We grip hands and hug with one arm.

"It was only a matter of time."

"Have a seat?" Kamal drops into a chair, and I sit beside him. "Y'all ready? This place will be packed."

"Today's Miya's day. I'm just here to do what I can to help. What about you? It's been a long year."

"Shit…tell me about it." He rubs his neck. "I'm better now that Jayda and Reese are home, where they belong. She's planning the wedding, and our little family is about to double."

"Double?"

"Yeah, she's pregnant, but don't say anything."

"Word?"

"Man, yeah."

"Congratulations!"

I pull my boy in for a hug.

"What are we celebrating?" Emmitt stands in the doorway, looking at me.

"Kamal has some news." I clarify.

"Jayda's pregnant. But we're keeping it on the hush until she finishes the first trimester."

"Damn, man, you couldn't wait to multiply." Emmitt gives Kamal a hug. "This is wild."

"Tell me about it. I'm just hoping the baby comes after the summer camp."

"Either way, we'll get it done," I offer. "But wait, you said double."

"Jayda thinks it's twins. It runs in the family, and she said it's already different from her pregnancy with Reese."

"What the hell are you going to do with three damn kids, man?" Emmitt yells.

"Take care of them. Love them. *Shit*, have some more."

We laugh. Kamal sits behind the desk, and we take the two chairs. We talk about the camp a little.

"I sent the contracts with the insurance requirements. They'll handle the background checks and the staff." Kamal passes the documents over to Emmitt.

"What about my coaches and the guest players?"

"They'll need background checks as well, but I made sure that you get the final word on who's hired to assist you."

Emmitt beams. He's wanted to run this camp for years. Football kept him off the streets, and he wants to give the same to the young boys in Houston.

"How much is it going to run us?" Emmitt asks, rocking forward in his seat.

DEK Ventures is paying for everything—the staff,

new equipment, uniforms, meals, everything down to the field's maintenance.

"Don't worry about it. We have it covered. Finish the season strong, and we'll discuss the details in a few months," Kamal says.

"Look, we need to hit Q's place tonight for drinks. But for now, I need to get to the kitchen." I stand up and pound with each of them. "Miya might need something."

"I bet she does." Emmitt laughs.

"What's that supposed to mean?" Kamal's head jerks between Emmitt and me.

"Nothing, D got it covered."

I shake my head. "I'm out."

"Nah man, what does that mean?" Kamal calls out, and it's muffled in Emmitt's laugh.

I reenter the office. "Emmitt, give us a second."

"Oh no, I'm sitting my ass right here."

"What's this about?" Kamal stands, crossing his arms over his chest. His chest swells as he stares straight into my eyes.

"Me and Miya," I tell him straight up. "I love her, and I asked her to marry me."

"*This muthafucka…*" Kamal rounds the desk, and Emmitt stands between us. "I told you not to touch my sister."

"Man, for the record, I didn't touch her. She touched me."

Kamal is trying to grab me, and I'm blocking. Emmitt's stuck in the middle, somewhere between furious and entertained.

"Imma kill him." Kamal reaches for my shirt, but I'm too quick.

"You're not about to keep reaching for me," I state.

Kamal and Emmitt exchange a glance and stare back at me.

"You can be pissed, but that's my woman."

Steam shoots from Kamal's ears, and I laugh.

"Laugh if you want to, you break my sister's heart, and I'm busting your ass. Mark my words."

"Who's busting who's ass?" Quan asks, with Rashaad and Demetrius standing in the doorway.

"*Fuck me...*" Miya's bullshit insurance.

"You gotdamn right." Kamal reaches, and I dodge him again.

"This fool's feet are faster than Muhammad Ali." Q howls.

"Dean hooked up with Miya." Kamal blurts out.

"What?" Q spins around like he's possessed. "Move, Emmitt."

"What are y'all doing?" Miya calls over the commotion.

"Handling your little boyfriend. I told you his ass was following her," Q says.

Miya weaves under Q's arms, slides past Emmitt, and stands between Kamal and me. She points a fork at him.

"Kamal, I have over one hundred people coming to eat. I need to cook. I don't have time for this."

"Baby Miya…"

"I mean it. Dean and I are together. That's that."

"No, it's not," Kamal states.

"Yes. It. Is."

"What the fuck she supposed to do with a fork?" Q mumbles.

Emmitt laughs. "Bruh, my thoughts exactly."

"I'm about to fork all y'all asses. Q, Rashaad, and Demetrius, Kamal will see you in the dining room in five minutes. Emmitt, either help or come back at three. Kamal and Dean, sit."

I kiss the back of her neck to ruffle Kamal's feathers.

"And keep your kisses to yourself. You came in here provoking him after I told you to wait. But you had to say something," Miya says while the others follow her orders.

"There goes Kamal's kingdom," Q teases. "Baby Miya has officially left the building."

"Damn right," she says.

"Don't sit," I tell her. "We can handle it from here."

"No, Dean."

"Yes, Miya. Start cooking, and I'll be right there." She swings the fork between us. "Behave. I love him, and I love you. Don't make me stab you with my good fork."

And on that note, she leaves. Kamal and I stand facing each other.

"Man, that's my sister."

"And she's my lady."

He grabs the back of his neck and drops in the chair. "Are you serious?"

"As serious as you are about Jayda and Reese."

Kamal looks up.

"I know Miya's more like a daughter than a sister. We played by your rules until we finished the project. Now, I want to freely express my love for her."

"So, you're asking for my blessing."

"No, I'm asking you to respect me, man-to-man. You know me, and I wouldn't say it if I didn't mean it."

"And you want to marry her."

"Yes."

"She wants a big wedding."

"She'll have it."

"And kids."

"She'll have them too."

He nods and opens his mouth.

"There's no need for threats. I wouldn't break her heart because it would be like breaking my own."

I extend my hand to my best friend, and I'm relieved when he takes it. We hug, and he slaps my back with two solid thumps. My spine rattles, but I get the point.

"Treat her right."

"No doubt."

"And come on," Miya yells from the hallway.

"You're supposed to be in the kitchen," Kamal yells back.

"And who's supposed to protect Dean?"

I laugh. "So, I need protection?" I ask her, opening the door.

"I told you I have four big ass brothers."

I shake my head, pulling her into my arms. I kiss the inside of her neck, glad to have this talk done.

"Let's get started."

"Actually, head to the kitchen. I'll be there in a few minutes," Miya says.

"You sure?" I ask.

"Yes."

I kiss her softly on the forehead and leave them alone.

. . .

DEAN LEAVES, and I stare at my brother. Kamal is more like a father than a brother. He practically raised me. I decide to start with gratitude.

"Thank you for always having my back, even when I didn't appreciate it." I drop in the seat beside him, taking his hand in mine. "It took living away from you to see that I missed having your protection. But I needed it to see that I can fly solo and still be all right. I might be battered and a little bruised, but I'm wiser."

Kamal's eyes glaze over, and he pulls me to him. "I'm so proud of you."

"And you and Dean will be all right?"

"Yeah, that's my brother. Brothers fight. And I'll table my ass-kicking for a future date." He kisses my forehead and sits back. "So, no more Baby Miya?"

"Nah, I'll always be your Baby Miya. But here, I'm Chef Miya. I've worked hard to prove to you that I can run this kitchen. Let me do what you're paying me to do."

"You got it." He smiles, and I see this is hard for both of us. "And I got you."

"I know." I hug Kamal again, resting my head on his chest. This man means the world to me, and I'm a blessed woman.

"Knock, knock."

"What?" Kamal yells.

"Babe, you good?"

I snicker, and Kamal shakes his head.

"Yes, Dean, I'm fine."

"You act like you're about to do something," Kamal yells.

"It's whatever," Dean yells back.

"Miya, what did you do to my boy?"

"Gave him some." I wink.

His eyes round. "I'm about to be sick. Get out."

I jump up laughing. "Love you, Big Boy."

"Love you too, Baby Miya."

I open the door and fall into Dean's arms.

"Love you, brother-in-law," Dean teases.

"Y'all ain't married yet. Now get started. We have guests on the way."

Dean turns, and with a pat on my ass, we're off. I look back once more at my Kamal and whisper, "Thank you."

"You're welcome."

CHAPTER 17

I CHANGE MY MIND. I'm back in my office sitting at my computer. Thinking of all the decisions that led to this moment. My fingers run over the keys typing up a revision to today's menu. The brunch series wasn't the test. Recreating the menu and making the experience my own—our own—posed the greatest challenge of my career and my life.

After talking with Kamal and surrendering to my feelings for Dean, I want to do something different. Something unexpected. I want to give our guests an experience.

"Baby, are you watching the time?" Dean stops in the doorway.

I thought I didn't need him, and in a lot of ways, I don't, but in so many ways, I do. He's been a rock, here like he promised, not standing over my shoulders but my man standing beside me.

He's constantly reassuring me that I'm good enough and I have this covered. And I know it for myself, but it never hurts to hear.

"Are you nervous?" I throw his question back at him, and unlike when we started this little project, I don't feel the need to prove myself.

This is my kitchen, and I'm about to show them what I can do.

"I'm not, but that might change if you don't get off the computer and start cooking."

"I want you to look at this." I pass him a printout of tonight's selections. "It's time to take Southern Soul to the next level."

"This isn't the menu we spent weeks arguing over." His brows shoot up, and he tilts his head back. "What is this?"

"You said something, well, a lot of somethings that hit me. And I think instead of serving a little of this and a little of that, I want to give our guests an experience."

A smile covers my man's face as he sits on the edge of the desk. "I'm listening."

"I want to give them the feeling of having an old school Sunday dinner. Family sitting around the table. One meal—two types of meat, four sides, fresh bread, and one dessert. The attraction is not the food, but the people."

"What do you need me to do?"

"Ready to roll up your sleeves and break a sweat?" I set the printer to create the menus.

"All you have to do is say the word." He leans over and smacks a kiss on my lips. Then he removes his jacket, and I'm momentarily taken by the turn of events.

Everything about my life feels like a blessing on top of a blessing. My relationship with my mother is stronger. My siblings and I are about to usher our family business into a new season based on old fashion family values. And I found love.

Me. Baby Miya.

And I've managed to not shed a single tear, until now.

"Wait…what's going on here?" Dean helps me up to my feet, and I snuggle into his chest.

"I'm overwhelmed with gratitude."

"Uh…but baby, you haven't cooked yet. Save the waterworks for after the meal is on the table." He nibbles on my neck and slaps my ass.

"Fine. But call my brothers. I want them to rearrange the dining room."

"We don't have time for that."

I kiss his lips. "Baby, what Miya wants…"

"...Miya gets."

I double pat his chest and slip on my apron. The menu is simple, with the addition of a new signature dish. I cover my hair with a net and shove my buds in my ears. I search my playlist and find the perfect song.

"No buds, babe." Dean points to the speakers he installed.

"Suit yourself." I press play on *Got to Give it Up* by Marvin Gaye. I crank up the volume and enter my zone.

I dance frying chicken. Electric slide popping the macaroni and cheese in the oven. Every once in a while, I look over to see my man chopping and dicing. Then in true Miya-style, I demand a dance break.

Dean and I dance around the kitchen. And bless my man's soul, because he doesn't have a lick of rhythm, but it doesn't stop him from dancing.

I feel eyes on me, and I look up and see Kamal. A smile crosses his face, and he's not watching me but Dean. I stop, touched by the affection in his eyes for Dean.

Dean's startled by the change and sees Kamal.

Kamal's slight nod and the tip of Dean's head melts my heart. I have my guys aligned, and that makes me unstoppable. They hug, and the next thing

I know, Kamal's rolling up his sleeves and grabbing an apron.

"Looks like you're about to break the pact," he whispers to Dean.

What pact? I wonder.

Then Jayda enters the kitchen, determined not to miss the party, and starts bumping and grinding with Kamal.

"Miya Miya."

"Hey, Reesie Piecie. Let auntie see what you got."

Reese dances on every inch of available space. My girl tears up the floor with her skirt twirling and her arms are in the air. Hopping around without reservation.

"Get it, baby! Your auntie don't know nothing about that move. Show her how we do it." Kamal hypes her up, and she gives him the show he's asking for.

And just when I think I can't take the cuteness, Lillian joins them.

"Pick us up, Daddy," Reese says to Kamal, and he scoops them up.

I look up to see Mamma and Daddy standing in the doorway of the kitchen. She's crying into Daddy's chest, and he's barely holding it together. This is what family's all about.

Everyone's caught up in the moment. Even

Demetrius is doing a little two-step with Catrina. I can't help but search the room for Rashaad, and he's now holding Lillian with his eyes on Cat.

Dean pulls me back to him and kisses my neck. "I think I caught my dream."

And now I'm crying. He smoothers me in his arms, and before we hit another repeat, the consultant hits the pause button.

"That's enough, dancing. We have guests coming. *It's game time, family!*"

THREE HOURS LATER, I close the oven after checking on my cobbler. I turn around to call out to Dean and see Mamma.

"What are you doing here?" I yell over the music.

"I'm here to help."

"No, ma'am, it's my kitchen today."

"But..." She walks over to the stove, and I block her, pointing to the door. "Miya Denise Montgomery."

She glances over my shoulder. "Why do they get to stay?"

Dean and Kamal assist me with preparing the food. The joy of seeing my man and my big brother tear the kitchen up has been the best reward for my hard work.

I kiss her cheek. "We'll explain later. Have a seat, and we'll be out shortly."

My mother drags her feet across the kitchen, and she's not the only Montgomery I have to kick out.

"Time to shower and change," Dean calls out, keeping time. "Q has the servers ready, and the dining room has been rearranged."

"Eeeekkkk. It's almost showtime. Don't let my peach cobbler burn." I run to the office to use the private shower and change. I rehearse my speech like I repeated my introduction because I don't want to miss a single word. Then I step out of the back and enter the kitchen.

Dean stops. "Turn around for me."

I spin around in my royal purple jacket, and I wiggle my ass because I know he likes it. He ushers me into the kitchen where the team is waiting.

"Chef Miya, your staff is ready." Dean steps aside, and I step forward, and the real work is about to begin.

CHAPTER 18

ALL THE CHAIRS are occupied in the dining room. The center table is decorated with platters of the food on tonight's menu. The waiters stand across the back of the room in royal purple uniforms, ready to serve individual plates.

Miya steps forward, and my chest warms with pride and love.

"Welcome to The Taste of Southern Soul." The guests clap. "About a year ago, Kamal decided he wanted to give this place a facelift. He knocked out walls, added new equipment, invited new members to our team. Then my brothers asked if I would accept the role as the head chef. I must admit my first thought was, *it's about damn time*."

They laugh.

"Then my second thought was I have some

mighty big shoes to fill. My grandmother cooked in that kitchen. My mother cooked in that kitchen. And one day, who knows, my daughter may cook in that kitchen." Her eyes glisten with unshed tears.

"Ahh, Baby Miya," Quan calls out, and that gets another round of laughter.

She sniffs. "So tonight I thought I'd make something very special for you. We have a family-style meal of fried chicken, fried catfish, baked macaroni and cheese, black-eyed peas, greens, cabbage, and hot-water cornbread. For dessert, I had a hard time settling on one. So in honor of my family, I made my mother's favorite peach cobbler, my father's favorite banana pudding, and Dean's favorite bread pudding with a vanilla whiskey sauce."

I didn't expect to hear my name. The bread pudding is a dish we mutually loved from Trios L'amour from our first night together. She recreated it with her own flair, adding whiskey and pecans. It's delicious.

All the eyes at the Montgomery table are beaming in my direction. Miss Jackie smiles, dabbing at the tears rolling down her face.

"The servers will bring out the food, and Kamal will bless it."

The room moves with commotion as the waiters bring out the plates. I'm answering questions, moving staff from the kitchen to the dining room when I find myself surrounded by the Montgomerys.

Miya's parents, Kenneth and Jackie, stand back. However, her brothers Kamal, Rashaad, Demetrius, and Quan are basically breathing down my neck when Miya bursts into the kitchen.

"What's going on?"

I stop her. "Let me talk with them."

"You have three minutes." I shake my head. "We have guests. No one likes cold food."

"Mr. and Mrs. Montgomery, guys, I'm in love with Miya. One day, if she lets me stick around, I hope to make her my wife."

There's a collective gasp, but no additional death threats. I count this as progress.

I pull her to me and look out at her family. "I know we're on a tight schedule, but for every restaurant I restore, help start, renovate, I carry a piece of this family. You guys showed me what it means to stick together, and I'll never be able to repay your generosity or thank you enough for sharing such an amazing woman with me. From the bottom of my heart, thank you."

They all nod, and I think I'm in the clear until Q says, "Did you tell him about the bullshit insurance?"

The room erupts with laughter, and Miya whispers, "Welcome to the Montgomerys."

I ROLL over and place a trail of kisses across Dean's chest. He cooked, cleaned, entertained, and came to near blows with my brothers. But he never left my sight, and I never thought I'd find someone that would cheer louder for me than my family, but Dean Wellington is a keeper.

"Dean…" I whisper.

"You can't possibly be awake." A sleepy smile crosses his face.

"Wanna dance?" I sit up. "I can't sleep."

After the dinner, everyone voted, and I'm officially the permanent executive chef of Southern Soul, starting at the top of the year. I've decided to tag along with Dean to complete his project before he moves back here.

"Now?"

"Yes, now." I toss back the covers.

"We're naked."

"That's what makes it so much fun." I stand with the carpet tickling my toes. Dean looks equally excited and confused. But my heart is full of love, and my soul is overflowing with gratitude. I have to dance off this energy.

I crack the blinds to examine his chiseled body in the moonlight.

"Do we get music?" he asks.

"You have the music in here. Just go with the flow." I place a hand on his heart, and we move. Swaying our body from side to side until I feel the heat of his body against mine.

We move as one, and we kiss. The type of kiss that makes the world stop spinning. That demands and promises and dares in the same breath. A kiss that reaches down deep, and I know that one day, this man will be my husband. I will have his babies. We'll build a life together.

We dance until I'm pressed against the wall, and Dean is inside me. Both of us anxious and beyond the point of no return. I scream his name, and he demands more, branding me as his own.

Dean groans my name, biting the tender flesh at

the base of my neck, as he delivers long strokes, smacking the ass he loves so much.

The intensity of our lovemaking sends us over the edge until we drop exhausted, dripping in sweat, begging for sleep to find us.

My eyes bounce, heavy under the weight of my day.

"Miya…"

I roll over, snuggling so close I smell the salt on his skin when I feel Dean slip something on my finger.

I gasp.

"I asked once but didn't have the ring. Miya Denise Montgomery, will you do me the honor of being my wife."

"Yes." I kiss him and ask the next logical question. "When?"

"Today, tomorrow. Plan the wedding of your dreams. But don't wait too long. I'm ready to shoot up the club, and I can't until you're officially Mrs. Wellington."

"Yes, sir."

We seal it with a kiss, and his love fills me from my head to my toes.

Kamal sent me on a journey to recreate our menu, but I've found so much more. I found the heart of Southern Soul—a new appreciation for family and how food brings people together. I found the soul in soul food. Unfortunately, I'm not at my goal weight, but I'm at my goal *me*. And thanks to my handsome man, I've found love.

Tears fill my eyes, and I can't stop them. Relief, happiness, joy all swirl in my body.

"Ahh, Baby Miya." He pinches my nose, and I smack his hand.

"I love you, Dean." I hold up my hand to see the ring sparkle, and a warm glow of joy flows through me.

"Love you too." He kisses me, and I stare into his smoky eyes. "Hey, baby…"

"Hum." I glance over at him.

"What's hide the pickle?"

I laugh, crawling over him until I'm straddling his sexy body. He runs his hands up my thighs, and I'm so glad this perfect man is all mine, and I'm all his. Now it's time to really have some fun. "Let me show you."

Thank you for reading **ALL YOURS**. Miya and Dean found their happily-ever after. Please take a few minutes and **leave a review**. I'd love you for life. :)

Thanks for all the emails about the next Montgomery story—Rashaad and Catrina are next. I think we need to have a Montgomery wedding.

Who should it be Kamal and Jayda or Miya and Dean? Email me at info@janesedixon.com! I'd love to hear from you.

PreOrder Your Copy!

Be the FIRST to know!

Join My Newsletter
http://www.janesedixon.com/subscribe

Be the first to know about releases and specials. You can unsubscribe anytime.

Rules are meant to be broken, and when it comes to love, this ex-quarterback and single mother are playing to win.

Kamal Montgomery owned the football field, and now he's one-fifth of Southern Soul, a family-owned soul food restaurant. Nothing and no one is off-limits until Jayda enters his restaurant in need of a second chance.

Jayda Dallas returns to Houston with her baby on her hip and her ex in the dust. He refuses to pay child support for their third-year-old daughter, and rather than take his sorry ass back, she's getting a J-O-B.

Jayda stands back, watching women fall at Kamal's feet. His smile is more deadly than his arrogance. But seeing him with her daughter has her wondering if she should take a chance.

Every rejection will only make Kamal's victory sweeter. He plans to lick, taste, and devour her like the delicacy she is until the world, her ex, and Jayda knows his name is tattooed on every inch of her curvy body.

Kamal's never played a game by halves, and Jayda's got a thing or two to show this deviously handsome player. But when an unknown enemy wages war on their budding relationship will their new love survive.

**Get Your Copy on Amazon
or Read in Kindle Unlimited!**

GOLDEN RAYS CUT through the curtains below eye level, casting a faint shadow over my beauty room. Time is passing faster than I can record today. Rocking forward, I flick the blinds a little wider, turning my head to the side, dodging the direct glare of the last hint of the day. I need the light to finish my last video for the week.

The national cosmetic brand paid me five grand to shoot this makeup look for my YouTube channel. The red light signals the camera is recording, and I pick up the fluffy contour brush.

I stare at the camera. "Drugstore makeup can deliver a comparable look to high end makeup if you use the right technique. Watch as I use this foundation as my bronzer." The brush glides over my naturally high cheekbones. The rich brown powder blends with the rose gold highlight.

"Mimicking an 'e' shape will bring the eyes to the center of your beautiful face." I say to my viewers with my eyes on the mirror. Like a trained makeup artist, I dust across my forehead, paying close attention to my temporal bones. My viewers love educational videos and tutorials, throwing in quick tips for help. "And don't forget the little area between the bridge of your nose and your brow bone."

I work quickly because I need to edit this video tonight after Reese goes to sleep. I have this video and four others lined up to publish on my channel while I'm in Houston taking meetings with potential brands with my boyfriend Brett.

In less than five minutes I'm applying my signature natural lip, racing the sun. I reach for my finishing spray.

"Mommy." The door to my beauty room pushes open, not wide enough for me to see in the monitor.

That's my girl. I smile, angling my head to the side, blocking the view from the camera.

"Honey, can Mommy get ten minutes?" Reese peeks around the corner and I hold up both hands, wiggling my fingers, and she nods. "Here, sit with me, they love when you're in my thumbnails." I pat the bench.

She skips through the door with a delightful smile on her face. I can tell she's adding a little extra effort to make her hair fall over her shoulders based on the click-clacking sound of the wooden beads on the end of her braids.

She jumps to an abrupt stop, giggling as the beads slap around. I scoop Reese up and sit her beside me.

"Can I have lip gloss?" She wiggles, getting comfortable while inspecting the makeup and brushes spread out in front of us.

I cut an eye at her. My baby is a genius. I know I'm biased, but she only has to see and hear a thing once to input it into her overactive imagination. It's a task to stay a few steps ahead of her quick wit. She pairs times and sequences with the ease of an older child. At least, I think so, since I had next to no experience with children until I had her. So, we're both learning as we go.

"Yes, but quickly, honey." I kiss the top of her head and rub off the pink residue. Reese yanks open her special drawer in my vanity and digs out her tube of gloss. I smile, watching as she applies it with focus and a steady hand. My nod of approval has my baby beaming as she returns to her drawer for a coloring book. She works on the end of my vanity and I return to finishing my look.

Reese understands makeup is for mommies only.

But she also knows I keep special items in the top drawer to keep her occupied while I work. Her favorite item is no doubt her tube of strawberry gloss.

I used to tell her makeup was for big girls only, then we started referring to her as a big girl for going to the potty on her own. My little genius asked within days if she could wear lipstick. I had to think quick, and that's when "we" created Mommy Rules. The first being, lip gloss is for big girls, and makeup is still for mommies.

As a full-time YouTuber, people used to drag me in my comments for letting my daughter wear "make-up." But I block them without a second thought. I draw the line concerning Reese. No if, ands, or buts about it.

What they'll never understand is the power that comes with embracing your beauty. It's not the lipstick or the gloss, but the whisper of confidence that comes with knowing you're the shit, and can't nobody tell you different, even when I find it hard to embrace.

My mother never told me I was beautiful. All I heard was my skin was too dark, my lips were too big, my hips were too wide. I was too much in her eyes. But I can't recall her ever calling me beautiful.

I took to beauty products, hoping to change my

appearance with the magic of makeup. Then I worked up the courage to sit in front of the camera.

I started teaching my viewers how to use makeup instead of going under the knife. Pouty lips without fillers. Snatched noses without rhinoplasty. Chiseled cheekbones without surgical sculpting.

It took one video going viral to change my life. More views garnered more attention. More attention brought on more admirers. And I found myself with fans that embrace my ethnic features because I learned to love my wide nose, my full lips, and my striking facial structure.

But in this house, and with Reese, I tell her she's beautiful, inside and out, every single day. Because no one ever told me, except for men interested in my body.

I stop, looking in the mirror. Time to take a few pictures. I face the camera.

"Gems, this is the final look. This is a great base to glam up, or for a beginner playing in makeup. Make the eye more pronounced for a night out with your man or use a bolder lip for drinks with your girls. We're out." I glance down at Reese, who's closing her book, and back to the lens to give my signature sign-off. "And remember Gem, makeup doesn't make you beautiful. You're gorgeous because

God made you that way." I wink and give a flirty goodbye wave with my fingers. "Toodles."

"Let me see." Reese stands on the bench with her glossy smile. Her golden skin mirrors her father but her eyes, nose, lips, are all me. "Gorgeous!"

"Thank you, Reesie Piecie. Now let's take this thumbnail." I switch the camera off video to take our picture and pass her the remote. "Ready?"

She nods, hiding the thumb size remote in her little hand. Reese will never doubt her beauty or her worth, and she'll never need a no-good man to tell her she's absolutely perfect.

"Need me to count."

"No, ma'am." Reese stares into the lens like a professional.

"Well, all right then, honey. Let's give them some face."

The camera chimes with the capture of each picture. Reese hits them back to back, giving us time to make slight moves. But we never take our eyes off the camera.

"Silly pose!" Reese squeals. I expand my cheeks like a human blowfish and cross my eyes. "Mommy…" She laughs with a squished face capturing the final picture.

Our laughter echoes through the house. I'm thrilled because we beat the sun. Now that's how to end a night of work. And suddenly the sweetest form of happiness settles over me. To think I never wanted children, but life gave me what I needed, Reese Dallas Hardin—my four-year-old clone.

"How about pizza for dinner?" I close the blinds and turn the camera off.

"And chicken?" Reese drops the remote into my side drawer.

"Yes, I'll order wings too. But you need to take your bath first. Deal?"

"Deal."

"Then chop chop, honey." Reese jumps down and I follow her down the hall with a full face of makeup like I have somewhere to go. But this is my life. Recording videos as an influencer and taking care of my number one priority, Reese. "Get your pjs and I'll start your water."

"Strawberry bubbles, please."

"You got it."

Reese disappears into her bedroom across the hall. It's only seven. I wonder if Brett will make in home in time for dinner. I sit on the edge of the tub pouring in the liquid bubble bath. The sweet fruit fragrance fills the bathroom, and I smile, emptying the basket of her favorite toys into the sudsy water.

"Don't forget your shower cap." I call out, pulling out my cellphone and opening the Message app.

My fingers fly over the screen. *We're ordering pizza and wings. Want your usual?*

I suck in a quick breath, holding my phone. The muscles in my fingers tense from my tight grip. My chest burns from the lack of oxygen, so I exhale until my shoulders buckle. The weight of trying to make our little unit a family is making itself known.

Deep down I know Brett's answer, but that doesn't stop me from hoping that this time I'm wrong. That he'll pick us over his entourage, his boys, and the owner of the pink panties.

"Mommy."

I jump, startled by her standing in the doorway with her nightshirt gathered to her chest. "Yes, baby."

"I need help." I help her out of her clothes and into the tub.

"I'll be right back." I slip out and grab my makeup wipes.

Multitasking is the name of the game in this house. I work around Reese's and Brett's schedules. I'll wash off this makeup and get back to editing the footage after she's in the bed. Before I reach the bathroom, I order the food after checking my messages for Brett's response once more. And true to his nature, there's nothing.

Somehow, we've found ourselves in an awkward "friend zone." It seems no matter how hard I try, or how hard I plead, we're stuck. We live in the same house, share the same bed, yet we live separate lives.

Brett parties all night and sleeps most of the day. I sleep through the night to wake early to care for our child. The moment she's off to school I work to build my relationship with cosmetic and lifestyle brands. Which went nowhere until Brett connected me with his team. His name wiggled me past the gatekeepers.

Thanks to their efforts I work around the clock. They got me on the public relations list for every major brand. I can barely review all the products I receive, even with recording from sunup to sundown. Hence this trip. His help shifted me from buying products with my money to receiving paid product placements and potentially brand deals. Brett gave me exactly what I wanted but the skeptic in me wonders why, and whether the pink lace panties have anything to do with it.

I turn out the light in Reese's room and hurry down the hall to get my wipes. When I stop at the sink, I chuckle at her splish-splashing in the tub before dropping my phone on the counter and facing my reflection.

For a quick tutorial it turned out well. I lean closer, inspecting my face. Dark brown skin and makeup can be friends or enemies. One brand may cause my rich hue to appear ashy, while another may cause my skin to radiate an inner glow. Overall, I'm pleased. I just hope the footage reflects the flawlessness finish of this soft matte glam look while I'm editing tonight.

Reese strikes up a conversation as I scrub away the layers—powder, foundation, blush, primer—that beautifully cover my imperfections. She flicks water around the bathroom, submerged in her rendition of her playtime fiascos. I don't trip over the small stuff. I'll clean it up after she's in the bed. Instead, I laugh and ask questions, allowing her animated story time to mask the imperfections of my life.

"Tomorrow you're going to Grannie Minnie's. How's that sound? Like fun?"

"Good."

"Yes, ma'am."

I lean over the sink to rinse my face, and I glance up at my bare face. "There you are," I whisper. The doorbell rings and I quickly dry my hands. "That's the food. Finish up, sweetie, so you can eat while it's hot."

I run out the bathroom and down the stairs. Living in a mansion never crossed my mind. My plan was to date for fun and snag a man who could take care of me. The older me laughs at the naivete of my younger self. It was on and popping until the pregnancy test came back positive. And in a flash, I thought my life had ended.

The team sidelined Brett due to an injury, and the pregnancy came at the right time. He had something to focus on other than himself, overlooking the extra pounds I put on and the change in our relationship. I went from a woman he showed off every chance he had, to the mother of his only child.

Ugh. I hate having my identity distilled to my reproductive organs. Almost more than I hate being his girlfriend for almost five years, or that he and Reese share the same last name. But on the flip side, I can't see forever with Brett.

Not like this. Not since the scales fell from my eyes twenty-three days ago—the moment I found a pair of lace panties in his Bentley. Panties, that don't belong to me. Panties that I would have missed if it wasn't for the circumstances surrounding our trip.

My car was due for a regular service appointment and my list of chores to prepare for staying a week in Houston had me coming and going in circles. So, I needed to drive his car. I stopped by the bank and went fishing in his armrest for a pen, and there I found them. Hot pink lace, folded, tucked away, damn near neon against the charcoal black interior.

I should be pissed. Right?

Throwing shit.

Cussing his ass out.

Reminding him I gave birth to his child.

Flaunting every stretch mark, my less than perky breasts, and my fuller hips. Reminding him of how he begged me to have Reese, to move into his house, and to make our situationship a family.

How can a slither of lace untangle the fabric of the life I'm desperately trying to hold together? I stop by the table in the front hallway and grab some cash for the tip from the drawer.

I guess… I stall for a moment, attempting to make sense of the unreasonable. But I guess I'm not pissed, because I'm not shocked. The panties, oddly, confirmed what I already knew. Brett and I haven't had sex in months. It's been so long I refuse to put a date to it, and if he's not getting it from me, he's getting it from someone.

I know.

I was that girl.

The girl who didn't care about a man's responsibilities at home as long as he kept me clothed in designer labels and rocking the most expensive handbags. But somewhere between giving birth to our daughter and finding those cheap-ass-lace-hot-pink panties, I realize I've changed.

Apparently, it took me four years to grow the fuck up and now the overwhelming question is… What do I plan to do about it?

I plaster a smile on my face and open the wooden

door. The delivery guy and I make small talk as he stacks scorching hot boxes in my arms. I bid him goodbye and hustle to the kitchen, placing them on the island.

Because the old Jayda Dallas would have told his ass to kick rocks. But the new Jayda knows it's not about me anymore. This is my baby's life too. So, instead of wilding the fuck out, like I wanted to do… like I want to… I swallowed my frustration with this relationship, my discontentment with my lack of autonomy, and I had a come to Jesus moment.

I prayed.

Prayed hard. So hard the sky parted and rained. I figure the Man upstairs had a good laugh at my expense.

Me, who had no regard for others. Me, who strongly considered whether to keep my child. Me, who has absolutely nothing to offer the world except my pretty face and makeup skills.

I spread the boxes out like a makeshift buffet, placing the roll of paper towels at one end and the pitcher of juice on the other. Then I pull down two plates, one for her and one for me.

Funny thing is, I didn't know when the shift began. Those panties make it hard to pretend I'm happy. That our relationship is the same. But what other choice do I have?

I cook and clean like normal. I record videos and smile for the camera. However, deep in my soul, I wonder if this is payback for the hell I've caused. I went from an independent woman to a woman with a child, living in his house, driving his cars. So, I brushed it under the carpet.

Then a few weeks ago, Milton, the new brand manager, invited us to Houston to meet with a few luxury boutiques. I jumped at the chance to fly back to Texas. Houston isn't home, but my best friend, Catrina, lives there. My hope, I guess, best case is Brett and I can rekindle our relationship. Worst case, Catrina and I can down a bottle of wine and help me get my shit together.

"Mommy."

"Coming and don't stand in the tub, I'm on my way." I take the stairs two at a time, stopping by the hall closet for a towel. I push the door open, and my heart drops. The sight of my child stops me dead in my tracks.

"Reese, how did you get bubbles in your hair?" I fight to hold back my laughter. We spent hours braiding her hair.

"I'm a princess."

"With a bubble crown?"

"Yes, ma'am."

I squat beside the tub, cupping her face in my

hands and kiss the tip of her nose. "Baby, the point of the shower cap is to not get your hair wet."

"Sorry, Mommy."

I help her up and wrap my strawberry-scented child in the fluffy towel. I made this bed and I wouldn't change anything if it means I'd have her. So, if it means stuffing my desires to give her a chance in life, with a mother and father raising her, I'll do it. She's worth it.

Ten minutes later, we're in the kitchen talking with our mouths full, when the hum of the garage door opening silences us. And I swear my baby shrinks in her skin. The sight wraps around my heart and squeezes me so tight I can't breathe. Then a car door slams.

"Eat, baby. It's getting late." I stand and kiss her forehead, not missing her slight tremble. Her stares at the door behind me. I turn her face to mine. "Want some juice?"

She nods, and I miss the light in her eyes. The mother in me wants to give her anything and everything that will make her happy. That's why I overlook the changes I see in Brett.

The late nights. The whispering phone calls. The broken promises. The side door opens, and he's startled straight.

"I'll talk to you tomorrow," Brett mumbles,

ending his phone call, stumbling a little. "Hey… my girls."

"Did you drive yourself home?" The stench of alcohol drowns out the smell of pepperoni. I stand beside Reese and she leans into me—by instinct I hold her. Brett stands taller, he towers over my five-and-a-half-foot frame, as his smokey eyes bounce between Reese and my protective arm around her shoulder.

"No, I came through the garage to keep from digging out my keys. What are you guys doing up?" He smiles down at Reese, dropping the device into his pocket.

"We're finishing up dinner. I'll make you a plate."

"Nah, I'm good, I ate with…" He stops himself.

The room falls deathly silent. I play the mediator between Brett and Reese. He regards her like an expensive possession, bragging about her and sharing her photos on social media. I know he loves her, but he's more like a friend than a father.

Which makes all my sacrifices seem futile. We stay because I want my daughter raised in a two-parent household. I want Reese to have a relationship with her father. Both are things I never had, and Reese deserves that and more.

"Okay… Then join us. Are you packed for the trip?" I sit and pull Reese's plate closer to her. "Milton sent over the itinerary for the week. We have a jam-packed schedule, but it should be fun."

"I need to lie down. Goodnight." Brett walks past us.

I glare at his retreating back. I have a choice here. Follow him or let it slide. Again. Then I look down at the tears gathered in my baby's eyes. The man's using her heart like a cheap trampoline.

"Daddy's just tired." She nods beneath my chin, as if she understands. But no child should understand his asshole ways. I want to follow him, but Reese comes first. "Finish your pizza and I have a special treat for you."

She sits back and smiles. "Cookies?"

"I don't know… maybe."

I squeeze her tight and give her a shake to make her giggle and her beads clang like windchimes. I walk over to the refrigerator and grab her a juice box. Then I do what I do best, change the subject.

"Want to stop and get some new coloring books?" I take a bite of my pizza, showing my baby how to brush it off. I'll have all night to process what just happened. But for now we'll focused on the next positive thing on her list and that's spending the next with Grandma Minnie, Brett's mother. She truly makes up for where her son falls short.

"One of those big ones like last time?" She loves the huge floor-sized coloring books.

"We'll stop by the store in the morning."

We finish dinner and clean the kitchen together. I get her to bed, and she's sleep within minutes. I exhale, mentally preparing myself for the second half of my day. It's time to edit, upload, and schedule all the videos I recorded today. I drag to my feet and flick on the soft purple nightlight, then I slip out, leaving her door cracked.

Reese sleeps like a rock. Once she's out, she's out. I chuckle, heading down the hall to my beauty room, and I surprised by the sound of Brett talking on the phone.

I glance at my watch—it's after midnight. He jumps a little when I yank the door open. "Would it have hurt you to sit and talk with her tonight? She missed seeing you all day."

"Don't start, Jayda. I'm exhausted."

"Not too tired to whisper on the phone." I gesture to his ever-present device.

A part of me wants to get it and see the evidence of all of his dirty deeds. But my pride won't let me do it. I promised myself the moment I turn into that woman, it's over. It's a shaky line, but it's all I got.

"Man, whatever." He rolls over in the bed, as if I'm not standing here. Then he glances back over his shoulder, "And since you're already bitchin', I'm not going to Houston."

"What? Then I'll stay home too." The words spill out, but this is a big break for me. For once, I'm carving out my own space and my own career, but it's not more important than my family.

"No, go. This trip is important. If you sign with these boutiques, more will follow."

"If it's so important, why are you staying here?"

"I'm meeting with a new potential client."

"A client?"

"Seems the word is spreading. I received an inquiry from another beauty blogger."

I can't see his face, but I hear the sarcasm in his tone. Brett was playing pro football when we met. Then he injured himself. After riding the bench, they let him go. Now, the very thing he used to laugh at is how I generate additional income.

He thought my YouTube channel was a joke until Milton approached me, and then Brett gave himself the title of my manager.

I had the followers and fans, but now I'm a brand with the verified blue checks and all.

"They'll expect to see my manager at these meetings," I remind him.

"Milton will fly out in two days. You can handle things for a few days?"

"I've handled things for years. So, you'll look after Reese? This would be a great time for you two to bond and..."

"No, my mom is looking forward to spending the week with her." He leans back against the headboard, staring at his phone.

I cross my arms. This picture is much clearer to me. His doggish ways know no boundaries. "And this will leave you plenty of time to do what you do."

"Quit tripping." He smiles, licking his lips before he completes the text message. Then he drops his phone onto the nightstand.

I stand in the dark, staring at his silhouette. All I can think about are those pink panties and the fact that I'm scheduled to remain in Houston for an entire week, and Brett will be here alone. He flips around a few times before settling, not bothering to look my way, or tell me goodnight.

Visions of panties and bras lingering over my house bombard my mind. He wouldn't... *Would he?*

Brett would. He'll have some skank in our bed before I can leave Reese at Minnie's house. And like a fool, I'm still with him. Still trying to make this dysfunctional unit a family.

I turn my head up to the ceiling, ready to plead with the Man above again. But why should He listen? I got exactly what I wanted: A man to match my swag. A man that is financially secure. A man every woman wants. A man that makes heads turn.

A man not ready to settle down, whispered through my head. And the old Jayda breaks through the haze of my uncertainty with a healthy dose of taught love.

Jayda, now might be the right time to wake the fuck up!

"SMELL THAT?" I rolled down my window and let the aroma of my mother's fried chicken fill the rented car. If it's possible for a scent to invoke the feeling of being home, it's my mother's food.

My mouth waters, signaled by the gurgle of my stomach, and for a brief second I hate I agreed to let Trish accompany me. We're stopping on the way to Los Angeles for a gathering with mutual friends. I suggested she visit the mall or check into the hotel without me, but she insisted on joining me for brunch.

My fingers wrap around the chrome handle and a wave of excitement ripples through me. My younger brothers—Rashaad, Demetrius, and Quan—and our baby sister Miya save a table inside since it's crowded.

I don't know which excites me more, seeing them or eating at Southern Soul.

I haven't visited home for more than a quick pop-in here and there since our folks remarried five years ago. And I haven't had my mother's chicken and waffles, or shrimp and grits, or…. "Come on, let's get going."

"You're taking me here?" Her wrinkled nose and displeased gaze say she's the fancy type.

I shake my head. Why didn't I leave her in New York? That's my bad for bringing her. Emmitt, my boy since college, introduced us, and I should have known something was up when he introduced us, instead of dating her himself.

I turn back to the old building, the unpaved parking lot, and the tasty cloud lingering out back over the smoker. The line wraps across the front side-walk and down the side, which I'd expect on a Saturday.

"Yeah, got a problem with it?"

"I guess not, but I expected…" Her eyes swept the area until her doe-like expression returns to mine. Then she hesitates, "It's fine."

I need to tell my boy Emmitt, Trish isn't my type. I like a woman that can hang in the hood, on the ski slopes, or at the governor's mansion, in the same day. My life covers it all, and any woman on my arm must adapt.

Timberlands. Stilettos. Flip-flops. I want it all, and stuck-up Trish may not make the cut.

I open the door, placing my feet on the land I know like I know the football field, like I know my own face because this place is home for me. I round the car, opening the door for Trish. We'll eat and head to do some shopping before flying out to Los Angeles.

I extend an arm to her, glancing into her eyes. This place is in the Fifth Ward in Houston. For most, it's the hood, but this is my old stomping grounds. Her heels crunch on the gravel as we approached the line. The old building seems smaller, a little more weather worn, and in need of a coat of paint.

"Yo, man, is that you, Kamal? What'd up with you?" A big man with a linebacker's build steps closer.

"Man, I can't call it. How's your family? And your folks?" Recognition settles the moment I hear Rodrick's laugh. We played ball in junior high and high school. We pound fists.

"Good. Good. Just trying to get in here and break bread with my ole lady. Can we get a picture with you? Been telling my lady I taught you everything you know on the field." His arm circles the woman beside him and pulls her forward.

"Taught me everything I know, huh? Still a bullshitter, I see." I smile, he's always had a large personality.

"Oh, then you know Rodrick well." The woman grins.

"Shut up Yvonne and take a picture with the man."

We share a laugh as the two bicker a little. I unfold Trish's hand from my arm and the two flank me.

I take Rodrick's phone and snap the picture, giving it back to him. "Don't forget to tag me."

"No doubt, man. Thanks. Wish the kids were here."

"Bring them by sometime. My number's still the same. I hop in and out of town."

"Word?" His eyebrows shoot up, as if surprised.

"I don't let this shit go to my head. We're still peoples. Now don't abuse it. But I'd love to meet your kids."

"Man, you were always my boy." He beams, stepping back in line.

"What are you up to now?"

He digs out a card and passes it over to me. "I have a private security company. We handle events, private detail, you name it I have a guy for your needs."

"I'll remember that." I slip the card in my pocket.

"Look, I gotta run. Enjoy your meal and thanks for the support."

We make our way to the doors. A few more people stop me while others frown. I stop at the podium, smiling at the hostess.

"Good morning, Catrina." Her lips curl into a welcoming smile and I return it. I pull out my phone to call my brother while I scan the crowd.

"They're waiting for you over there." Catrina points to the dining room facing the street.

"Wait, this is a group date?" Trish halts, causing us both to stop.

"I told you I'm here to check on my family. You still wanted to accompany me." I hold up a finger to my brother, Rashaad, and face Trish. I glance at my watch and drop my hands in my pockets. This "date" started five hours ago. She talked the entire ride over, name dropping to show me she's part of the "in crowd" in NYC. Now, I'm ready to eat and kick it with my sibling. I glance over and seeing all of them at the table makes me eager to find a solution with Trish.

"How about I call you a ride back to the hotel?" Then I sweeten the offer. "I can make us reservations and we can hit up a few spots around town later tonight."

The sour look glued to her face since we parked disappears. "That sounds more like it."

I pull out my phone to call a car service.

"No need, I got it." She tips her head to the waiting car. "You have my number, call me when you're ready." She sashays off without a glance back.

I shake my head and chuckle. I'm not surprised. She's here to be seen and not at a hole in the wall restaurant. Southern Soul is about rolling up your sleeves and devouring Southern comfort foods. There's nothing glamorous about it, just good food in a family environment.

"Yo, Big Boy, the biscuits are getting cold," Q calls out over my shoulder.

"Don't start that Big Boy shit with me." I stroll over to the table. My brothers and sister stand to greet me. We collide in a familiar huddle, then I give each my undivided attention.

"What the superstar is too good for his nickname?" Q and I execute our signature handshake, ending with a salute. Then I gather his big ass in my arms. "Man, stop!"

The others laugh while I rough him up. Quan was the baby for years until our folks surprised us with their *oops* baby, and the only Montgomery dressed in pink, Miya. I turn and face my baby that's not a baby but a grown woman.

"Baby Miya." Her arms circle my waist and I hold her tight. "I missed you, love."

Miya glances up with a smile. "Not enough to bring your player ass home. Who was that?"

"Nobody. Trying to multitask. So, what's the emergency that required flying home?" She steps back, making room for Demetrius, the middle child always quietly observing the world. "How's the book coming along?"

"Slow, but I'm not in a rush. What about you? Are you planning to stick around for more than the weekend?" Demetrius grounds me with a firm hand on the shoulder.

The thought of staying in the city more than a weekend means I'm bound to bump into Kenneth, and I'm not there yet.

"And your niece needs more than weekly Face-Time calls." Rashaad adds, stopping behind his chair.

Their expectant faces make me feel trapped yet grounded. Each standing behind a chair awaiting my response. Man, I miss my family.

I never thought I'd settled anywhere but Houston, but our parents remarrying changed everything. The fourth largest city in the United States isn't big enough for Kenneth and I to live.

"I'll see what I can do and tell my girl I'll be by to get her for a day of the works."

"She'll be packed and ready to go. Now let's eat." Rashaad laughs, taking the attention off me and back to food.

My chair is at the head of the table. I sit scanning the table and pride fills my chest—like a proud father. Each of my siblings are thriving and it shows. As the eldest of the five Montgomery children, I raised them like my own from the moment our mother signed the divorce papers. At thirteen I became the man of the house and I took my role seriously.

None of my siblings have seen the inside of a jail cell, although Q had a few close calls. None of them were teenage statistics. All of them are college educated and successful in their chosen fields.

"What's so important that y'all couldn't share it over the phone?" The collective shift of the energy sends a chill down my spine. "What is it? Is it Mother?" I guess since she's not here.

"You could say that." Rashaad flags down the waitress. "We're ready for our orders."

"Well, don't all speak at once."

A series of unspoken messages bounce between them until the ball drops in Rashaad's lap. He's the second oldest and the one that keeps me in the loop. My decision to live on the east coast following my retirement from the league put a wedge between us, and that's something I need to repair.

"The folks are ready to retire." Rashaad shrugs, leaning back with an arm resting against the table. The casual posture speaks volumes.

"And?" I grab a buttermilk biscuit from the basket and my stomach stirs.

"*And...* they want us to take over the restaurants." Miya bookends the announcement.

"It shouldn't surprise us. I just wasn't expecting it this soon." I glance around the room, seeing Southern Soul with fresh eyes. We were raised in this building. The school bus picked us up and dropped us off at the end of that gravel driveway.

The place once served cafeteria style, then we added waiters before I left for college. Then I had the place expanded when I landed a contract as a professional football player. We added windows to bring in more natural light and updated the restrooms and kitchen. But that was almost fifteen years ago.

"Kamal..." Q interrupts my musing. "This place isn't what it used to be."

"What do you mean? It's packed. There's isn't an empty seat in the dining room, and there's still a line outside."

"On Saturdays, but Monday through Friday it's a ghost town. Mom's not making enough to support the staff, let alone moving—"

"Moving?"

They share a grimace.

"They're ready to turn over the reins and sell the house too." Q says, the fidgety tap of his fingers captures my attention more than his words.

"Sell the house?" I turn to Rashaad. "Is it listed?"

"Not yet, but Mom's already consulted a stager and started removing our things."

"And what does *Kenneth* have to say about all of this?" I toss the biscuit back in the basket. "I'm sure this is all his idea. Probably filling her head with more of his fucking lies."

"Dad says it's her idea," Miya says.

"Yeah, right? To give up her home, her business, leave her children and grandchild behind. Sounds like more of his manipulation to me." I pinch the bridge of my nose. "It was only a matter of time. He wants to get her away from us. And then what?"

I want to stand up and walk the length of the room, but that's not possible. The last time I attempted to talk with Mother about her rekindled a relationship with our father, it was on their wedding day. She shut me down and told me it wasn't any of my business. I honored her wish to walk her down the aisle, but our relationship changed.

Now Kenneth and I respect each other's boundaries, and my mother's wishes. And our "conversations" are nothing more than common pleasantries, since he walked out on us twenty years ago.

"I think he's on the up and up," Q says.

"And you, Demetrius?" I glance over at him, sitting on the other side of Miya.

"He seems different. But I don't trust him."

"Rashaad?"

"I don't want to think the worse, but Mom's house is worth at least two million dollars. Two point five if we list at the right time."

I whistle, not realizing the house had appreciated in value over the years. But with the renovations we did for her birthday a few years back and the new construction in her subdivision, I'm not surprised. She owns a house inside the loop. People would pay a pretty penny to get their hands on that property, even if only to level the house and build something larger.

"So, you think he's trying to get in her purse?" My heart races like the moment a play is called on the field, as I contemplate my next move.

"Man, I don't know. But she always said she'd never leave Houston. Especially with me having Lillian." Rashaad has full custody of his six-year-old daughter after his nasty divorce last year.

"Miya?" I ask.

"I think he's changed. He's not the same man he was when we were kids." Her compassionate eyes plead with each of us, but Miya's always been a daddy's girl. "I think we should give him a chance. People change."

"When people show you their true colors, you paint that shit in ink." I chuckle, but nothing about this predicament is funny. I don't trust the man. He left us once, and I don't put it past him to do again. "The moment I believe Kenneth is different is the moment y'all can commit my ass to the crazy house. Have y'all talked with Mother, alone? And why is this the first time I'm hearing about this?"

"Mom's an adult. I make it a point to stay out of her personal affairs." Rashaad lifts a hand in the air in resignation. "I figured she'd tell you when she's ready. As for this meeting, we called you in because of our growing concern for the restaurant."

I glance around at the business in question, not pleased with being left in the dark about this matter. I open my mouth to respond and see the waitress approaching the table.

I sit back to give her room. She places the plates of food on the table while I mull over the news. Our parents were joint owners. During their divorce they agreed to split the business in half, while keeping the Southern Soul name intact.

Southern Soul Houston went to Mother, and

Southern Soul Raleigh went to Kenneth. I haven't visited the Raleigh location since my early teens, and the effect of their remarriage on the business never crossed my mind. Not when the business documentation has us listed as equal owners. Therefore, any significant changes would need the majority approval of each of us. That fact gives me some relief, but our contracts mean nothing if Kenneth is playing with my mother's heart.

A plate blocks my vision for a moment. The corners of my lips turn up as the scent of my mother's signature spices tickles my nose. The oversized waffle covers the plate topped with four perfectly fried chicken wings. Miya squeezes my hand, and I know she ordered.

"You're a real one," I tell her and grab my fork.

"You know it." Miya winks, slipping the utensil from my hand, and intertwines our fingers.

I almost forgot. I sit straight up and scan their faces, waiting for me. "Demetrius, will you bless the food?"

"Father…"

All heads bow. His words float in and out of my mind. He prays over the food, our family, over the decisions we must make. We end with a boisterous "amen." I linger for a moment, looking over my siblings.

"Rome wasn't built in a day, brother," Q calls out, smothering his scrambled eggs in salsa.

I nod and pick up my fork. I guess I need to shift my schedule and head over to Mother's to get to the bottom of this change. What I know without a doubt is Kenneth won't get his hands on Southern Soul Houston.

"Eat before it gets cold. You know how you hate cold chicken." Miya passes the hot maple syrup.

"Yes, ma'am." I take her offer and cover the piping hot food with a thick coating. I'll eat now and handle this situation later. I cut into the waffles, eager for nostalgia to settle in as the sweet batter melts on my tongue.

The food lightens the mood as we shift from family business to catching up on life. Lillian in elementary school. Rashaad expanding his real estate agency. Miya considering whether to move back home for good.

"I'm glad you finally dumped that jerk."

"I'm starting to think all men are jerks." Miya picks at her food.

"Damn, throw us all under the bus with his loser ass. We told you he was a player," Q says.

"Q, you belong under that damn bus. All of y'all, except Rashaad. Lining up women like trophies. One day, you'll find you match."

"Like you found yours," he teases. Q isn't one to hold his tongue and the two of them stay at each other's throats.

"Q, keep playing with me." She thrusts a fork in his direction.

"What are you going to do now?" I ask Miya.

"Look for a job here. I want to find a place I can stretch my creativity. Maybe become a head chef."

"I have a few connections in the city," I offer.

"Not now, I plan to take some time off. Hit the gym. Focus on myself for a change."

I exchange looks with Demetrius. I caught that "hit the gym" and he did too.

"Miya, there's nothing men like more than a sexy, confident curvy woman." I have two true loves and she's one of them. Knowing some no-good man has her doubting herself makes me want to find him and express my displeasure.

"Correction. Purchased curves. Not real ones."

"Baby Miya's on a roll." Q smiles, trying to get under her skin.

I wish I could reach him. Then I look at the next best thing. "Rashaad…"

Like a mind reader, Rashaad pops the back of Q's head and our laughter fills the room.

"Don't kill the messenger," Q barks, sliding away from Rashaad.

I wipe at my tears as he rubs the back of his head. That's when I see a beauty outside the bay window.

She steps out of a silver luxury car. Her brown skin so rich it looks photoshopped. The fitted business suit contours her curvy frame, stopping midthigh.

Sexy…

She spins around to gather her luggage, when her head tips back and I assume she's laughing at the driver. Her hair floats around her oval face and I smile, as if hearing it. Then she takes the offered business card, giving the driver a sultry smile, and my breath catches.

I lean forward, unable to look away as the driver stumbles a little, spellbound. I don't blame the brother. I freeze, watching the scene unfold until the driver pulls away. Then she turns, heading this way.

"Excuse me." I drop my napkin beside my plate and head out to meet the black beauty. She's rolling Louis Vuitton luggage over gravel like it's smooth concrete.

"This ninja is always recruiting," Q says behind me, but I'm focused on the door.

I stroll through the crowd and out the door. She turns, mumbling at the luggage, lowering until she tilts her curvy backside in the air.

I see you, baby… I don't stop until I'm beside her. "Let me help you with that."

Continue Reading…

**Get Your Copy on Amazon
or Read in Kindle Unlimited!**

Blazin' Love (Contemporary Romance)

Complete Series

Platinum Love (Book 1)

Privileged Love (Book 2)

Exclusive Love (Book 3)

Chosen Love (Book 4)

Special Love (Book 5)

Absolute Love (Book 6)

Pretend for Me (A Short Story)

Devoted Love (Book 7)

Select Love (Book 8)

Lavish Love (Book 9)

Total Love (Book 10)

Forbidden Chords Series (Contemporary Romance)

Complete Series

Hidden Desire (Prequel)

Rockstar Seduction (Prequel)

Rockstar Secrets (Book 1)

Rockstar Sinners (Book 2)

Rockstar Savages (Book 3)

Waiting for You (A Short Story)

This Song's for You (A Short Story)

Rockstar Scandals (Book 4)

Precious Stones Series (Romantic Suspense)

Before Black Diamond (Prequel)

Black Diamond (Book 1)

African Emerald (Book 2)

Fire Opal (Book 3)

Southern Gentlemen (Slow Burn Steamy Romance)

Play to Win (Book 1)

All Yours (Book 2)

Honest and True (Book 3)

Smith Pact Duo (Contemporary Romance)

Complete Series

Yuki's Luck (Book 1)

Tempting Asher (Book 2)

Smith Surprise (Book 3)

When It Comes to Love Boxed Set (Books 1 - 3)

Weekend Reads

Resort to Love

You Owe Me

Grown and Sexy for Christmas

Standalone Novels

Her Last Man

See all of my books on my website:

http://www.janesedixon.com/books.

ABOUT THE AUTHOR

USA Today Bestseller, Ja'Nese Dixon writes tales of romance laced with strong women, stronger men, and family values that based on more than blood. Her happily ever afters are written to inspire. So, if you're looking for a page turner that will leave you blushing, with your heart racing, and lying to yourself about reading "just one more chapter" then grab one of the author's thirty-something books.

Ja'Nese is an avid reader and coffee drinker living in Houston, TX with her husband, three adult children, and her spoiled diva dog. Want to learn more? Join her newsletter and get exclusive reads, all the inside details, and a first look at what's to come at www.janesedixon.com.

Stay in Touch:
www.janesedixon.com
info@janesedixon.com

facebook.com/AuthorJaNeseDixon

twitter.com/janesedixon

instagram.com/authorjanesedixon

amazon.com/author/janesedixon

bookbub.com/authors/ja-nese-dixon

Get Waiting for You for FREE!

Do you love second chance romances? Then here's another sweet, steamy romance for your device.

https://geni.us/waitingforyougift

9 781950 405282